SO I WAS IN JAIL

What I had feared all my outlaw life had finally come to pass.

I stared at the floor of my cell and made myself believe that it was not going to be long before I was a free man again. After all, I was tough. I'd been born tough, raised tough, and I'd stayed tough.

And I could take a jail cell; I could take it without cigarillos and whiskey. Shit, I could take it without food and water.

Goddammit, I was Wilson Young and I was a long ways from beaten.

Other books by
GILES TIPPETTE

FICTION

THE BANK ROBBER
THE TROJAN COW
THE SURVIVALIST
THE SUNSHINE KILLERS
AUSTIN DAVIS
THE MERCENARIES
WILSON'S GOLD
WILSON'S LUCK
WILSON'S CHOICE
WILSON'S REVENGE
WILSON'S WOMAN

NONFICTION

THE BRAVE MEN
SATURDAY'S CHILDREN

THE TEXAS BANK ROBBING COMPANY

Giles Tippette

A DELL BOOK

A DELL/ELEANOR FRIEDE BOOK

Published by
Dell Publishing Co., Inc.
1 Dag Hammarskjold Plaza
New York, New York 10017

Copyright © 1982 by Giles Tippette

All rights reserved. No part of this book may be
reproduced or transmitted in any form or by any
means, electronic or mechanical, including photocopying,
recording or by any information storage and retrieval
system, without the written permission of the Publisher,
except where permitted by law.

Dell ® TM 681510, Dell Publishing Co., Inc.

ISBN 0-440-18847-4

Printed in the United States of America
First printing—May 1982

*To Ann Wallace,
friend and partner*

Chapter One

We went down to Laredo from San Antonio without any intention of robbing any banks or doing any kind of outlawry of any kind. Hell, we had plenty of money from the robbery in Sabinas Hidalgo and the kind of short-changed job in Houston and we were more or less on holiday. I'd sent Marianne around on the train from San Antone, but me and my two partners had ridden our good horses overland.

Marianne was my woman, the kind of woman that damn few men ever get and near about none in my form of work. I called her my virgin whore, which was about what she was. She'd been a whore, a prostitute when I'd met up with her, but she'd renounced all that for me. She used to tell me she felt like I was the first man she'd ever been with. Which made her a virgin. But she knew every trick in the trade, such as a whore would. So I had the best of both worlds. She'd be waiting for me in Laredo with a room all set up in the Palace Hotel and all my wants seen to when I got there.

That summer morning, riding across the prairie with the sun just up and the air sweet off the sagebrush, it was good being alive, it was good being Wilson Young.

Even if I was wanted by every lawman on both sides of the border and was carrying enough money on my head to load down a pack mule. But I'd been lucky thus far and, like all fools—and all outlaws are just naturally fools—I figured I'd go on being lucky and making plenty of money and staying free.

I was thirty-four that summer and I'd been in the outlaw trade for half that time, ever since I'd drifted into it at the age of seventeen. It's said that all outlaws are misfits and mean and bitter men, but I never considered myself that, nor did I think of some of my partners that way. On my part I'd sort of drifted into the trade for lack of direction after the carpetbaggers and scalawags had robbed my family of their ranch holdings down around Corpus Christi, right after the Civil War. The loss had killed my daddy, and my mother had followed him shortly, leaving me, just a schoolboy, on my own with no trade and no other family to turn to.

In a sense, I reckon, partners had always been my family. I'd never given it much thought, but until Marianne, there'd been no kith or kin that meant anything to me except the men I'd rode and robbed with. They say that blood is thicker than water, but I couldn't vouch for that. I'd never had no blood kin that had gone in to some of the tight places me and my partners had survived, and I'd never had blood relations that I'd of trusted to watch my back the number of times I'd trusted partners.

THE TEXAS BANK ROBBING COMPANY

I guess what had put my mind onto partners was the fact that we were nearing Laredo and, of course, just across the border, Nuevo Laredo. And it was in Nuevo Laredo that the best friend and partner and maybe the finest man I'd ever know, Les Richter, had been killed. Killed by two bounty hunters, Morton and Bird. In my attempt to rescue him from an infirmary, where I mistakenly thought he was still alive, I'd nearly been killed myself, sustaining three gunshot wounds and only surviving through the unexpected kindness of two old Mexican women who'd hid me away for the weeks it had taken for my recovery.

But all that was many years ago, perhaps eight or ten, and like all misfortunes just as well forgotten.

Riding, I looked up at the sun, calculating it to be near two o'clock of an afternoon. It was hot, plenty hot, as it always is in that brush and cactus country except about two or three months out of the year. But we weren't minding the heat, for we were just going along, taking it easy. We had no special time to be in Laredo and nothing, really, to do once we got there. The little town of Encinal was between us and Laredo. I judged us to be fairly close to it, and I decided, rather than making the twenty odd miles we had to go to Laredo that day, we'd stop and drink a little whiskey in Encinal and rest up. Maybe go on after dark, depending on how we felt.

A little farther on I called a halt and we all got down. I rummaged in my saddlebags and got out a bottle of rum, took a drink, and pitched it to Wilcey.

Wilcey, Dennis Wilcey, and I had been together about five years. Outside of Les Richter, I considered him about the best partner a man could have. He was, however, a pretty unlikely candidate for the owl hoot trail. He'd been a rancher up in the Panhandle country before his wife had run off with another man, causing him to go to pieces and take to drink and almost ruin himself. When I'd met him he'd been a professional gambler in the border country up near El Paso. It had been me that had brought him into the outlaw business when he commenced his career by helping me rob a poker game in El Paso. I'd done that business of making an outlaw out of him out of gratitude for his saving my life.

Or, at least, that's the way he sometimes put it.

In a way he reminded me of Les. Not that they looked much alike, though both was tall and lanky. No, it was more that sardonic grin he wore most of the time and the way he had of hoorahing me with a straight face so that I never knew if he was after my goat or not. He wasn't nowhere near as good with a gun as I was—of course damn few was—and he worried a little too much for my taste, but he was still a damn good man and one that it would do to ride the trail with.

He said, "Where the hell are we, Will?"

"Lost," I said. "Where the fuck you think we are?"

"Aw, don't come that on me. How much futher we got to go?"

I squinted around me. Wasn't much in the way of landmarks. That country is all rolling plains full of cactus and rocks and sand. I said, "I figure we're a couple of miles from Encinal. I figure we'll hole up there for a few hours. That whorehouse might even still be there." I gave Wilcey a wink. "That is, if the Nigger Meskin will let us try it out."

The Nigger Meskin was Chulo, the meanest looking man I'd ever seen. We called him Nigger because he was so black, made even blacker by the stubble of beard that was always on his face and the black handlebar mustache that curled down around his mouth. I don't know what it was made him look so mean. He had a hooked nose and a knife scar over his right cheekbone, and it could have been that. Or it could have been the eye patch he wore over his left eye. He'd lost that lamp when he and I were robbing a train together about five or six years previous and a chunk of lead had ricocheted off a lock we were shooting off and lodged in his eye. I guessed it didn't matter what made the sonofabitch look so ugly and mean. I guessed all that mattered was he was my friend and recognized me as the boss, the *jefe*.

He said, "Say, Weelson. They got the whorehouse in Encinal?"

The sonofabitch would rather fuck than drink. In fact, I'd never seen anything he wouldn't fuck. Wilcey always said the Nigger would fuck a wildcat if he could find somebody fool enough to hold it.

I said, "Aw, Chulo, I was just funning you. They ain't got no whorehouse in Encinal. They ain't even got no women there."

He commenced to look worried. "No weemen?"

"No weemen," I said, mocking him. "Just shut up and drink some rum."

I was in a damn good mood. I felt like we was on some kind of holiday. I couldn't remember when the last time was I'd been going somewhere just for the hell of it, with no job planned or with no intentions of looking to search out a job.

We passed the bottle around one more time. I lit a cigarillo and said, "Well, let's go on into Encinal and get a little grub and see what the town has to offer."

Wilcey said, "Will, you sure we're doing the right thing? I mean, going down to Laredo."

Well, he was playing the old woman again, which he was damn good at. I said, "Goddammit, Wilcey, we got all this decided back in San Antonio. Now don't start it all over again."

Naturally he wouldn't let it alone. He said, "Well, I just don't see what was the point of leaving San Antone. We were doing just fine there. Wasn't anybody bothering us and I felt safe."

I said, wearily, "Wilcey, we were in San Antonio for two months. Wasn't you getting a little tired of it? I know damn well I was. Did you want us to stay there the rest of our lives?"

"Now you know that ain't what I mean," he said. "But we were doing all right there for the time being, and I think we ought to have stayed until we got ready to pull another job. Taking a risk for a job is one thing, but what the hell we going to Laredo for?"

"Because," I said patiently, "I want to."

"Aw, hell," he said. "I know better than that. You just want to take Marianne to Mexico because she ain't never been."

"That's part of it," I admitted. "But I kind of miss Mexico myself. That part of Mexico. It's been a damn good few years since I been in Laredo, and I always liked that town."

"It ain't safe," he said stubbornly.

I mounted up. "Wilcey, how many times do I have to tell you that there ain't nothing about this life that is safe. You keep forgetting we are in the outlaw business and not being safe is just part of it."

He was still on the ground, holding his horse's reins. "Yes, but some parts is safer than others. They ain't no point in taking unnecessary risks." He turned to Chulo. "Ain't that right, Chumacho?"

He was always doing that, appealing to Chulo when his arguments couldn't make no headway with me. It never did him no good. To Chulo, I was the boss and whatever I decided was what we did.

It was the same this time. The Meskin shrugged and said, "Weelson is the *jefe*. He pretty good for ol' Chulo. I do what he theenk."

"Aw, shit!" Wilcey said in disgust and stepped up in his saddle. "That goddam Meskin can't think for himself. Man, you got him fooled!"

Within an hour we'd raised Encinal out of the prairie. It was just a little clutter of buildings suddenly jumping up out of the hot prairie as we topped a little rise. I'd spent a little time in Encinal, though not much, for there really wasn't a hell of a lot of reason for anyone to be in Encinal. And as far as that went, there wasn't a hell of a lot of reason for Encinal to even be at all. It wasn't on the way to nowhere except Laredo, and it was just sitting out there in the middle of nowhere surrounded by nothing but cactus and rocks and a few stringy long-horned cattle. It was mostly saloons and eating joints and a fleabag hotel or two with a few Mexican whores thrown in for them that had a strong enough stomach. It was mostly occupied by some pretty bad hombres, and that may have been what kept it going. Not that it was a hole-up town. There wasn't any law there, but if outside law wanted you bad enough and they were strong enough, they'd come in and take you. But generally, a cattle thief or small-time bandit could feel safe enough there. Most of the cattle thieves that went down into Mexico and rustled cattle and drove them back into Texas pretty much made Encinal their headquarters. Then you'd run into a pretty good mixture of hard cases of all kinds. It wasn't the kind of town you'd want to go into if you had a wagon load of Sunday school books you wanted to peddle.

But we come riding on in good style and pulled up in front of a big adobe-and-log saloon and got down and loosened our horses' cinches and then went walking on in, our spurs jingling on the hard-packed dirt of the sidewalk.

The interior of the saloon was dark and cool, or at least it was cooler than it was outside. We stopped just inside the door to let our eyes adjust to the light change. Men in our line of work make a habit out of doing that, just to be sure everybody's friendly in the place before we go barging on in.

There was a long bar against the wall to our left and about ten tables scattered over the rest of the room. The place was just moderately busy. There was a poker game going on over in the back corner and three or four other customers scattered around at tables with a few more up at the bar. We went on over and took a table against the far wall. The bartender hollered over to ask what we'd have. I asked him if he had any good Mexican brandy, and he said he did so I told him to bring us a bottle on over.

Then we kind of settled down. I shoved a spare chair

away from the table and put my boots up on it. I lit a cigarillo, holding the lucifer match for Wilcey while he got one out and lit up too. There'd been a little gap of quiet when we'd come through the door, but now the talk had picked back up again. Now that I could see well enough I looked around, half expecting to see someone I knew, but I didn't recognize a face.

I said to Chulo, "See any *amigos,* Nigger?"

He looked around and then shook his head. His cousin in San Antonio was the main cattle buyer for stolen Mexican cattle, and I figured there was at least one hombre in the place had done some business with the cousin.

Chulo said, "Where the weemen?"

Wilcey and I laughed. "I told you, ain't no weemen."

The bartender brought our brandy and glasses over then, and I rung a twenty-dollar gold piece on the table and told him to keep the balance against what else we'd eat and drink while we were there.

I said to him, "You got any women here?"

He shrugged. He looked to be about half Mexican and half white man. He said, "Couple in the back. They don't much like to work during the heat of the day. Place down the street is a little livelier for that sort of thing."

Wilcey said, "What the hell you asking about women for? Hell, you got Marianne coming. She'll be waiting for you in Laredo."

There was a little edge in his voice and I understood why. He'd lost a woman in Houston, the first woman he'd really ever taken up with since his wife had run out on him. I knew it was still an open wound to him.

I'd hated that it had happened, even though I'd seen it coming. She hadn't been a good woman. Oh, I guess from the outside you'd have thought she was a nice respectable lady. But she was a one-eyed jack. She showed the world one side of her face, only we'd seen the other. We'd seen it when she'd run out on Wilcey and run out on us taking with her $30,000 from a robbery we'd pulled in Houston. I hadn't minded the money, but I had minded the hurt she'd done Wilcey. He'd been bitter at women for a long time on account of his wife, and then when he decided to trust another one, he had to pick a bitch that was going to run another red hot poker through his heart.

So that was why I didn't mind him saying that about Marianne. I said, "I wasn't asking about the women situation for myself, but for our son here. You know how he gets if he has to go more than three or four hours without a piece of ass."

Wilcey just grunted, not laughing at the joke. I knew women were going to be a sore subject for him for a long time.

We hadn't touched the brandy so I poured out all around, and then we all said "Luck" and then knocked them straight back as befits the toast.

It was middling brandy. But then poor brandy, to my mind, was better than the best rum. Which was what we'd been drinking the last few days, me having left the whiskey provisioning to Chulo and rum having been what he'd brought along.

The Meskin said, "We rob one Meskin bank?"

That sonofabitch was always wanting to rob a bank in Mexico. I never could figure that out. I shook my head. "No, we don't rob one Mexican bank. We don't rob no banks this time."

Wilcey said, "By the way, how much longer we going to lay off? We ain't got all that much money."

Well, that wasn't true. We had a little better than $8,000 a man and, even the way we spent, that should last a little while.

I said, "Oh, hell, let's don't worry about it for right now. Let's go on and have a good time for a while."

He said, "That don't sound like you. Ever since I've known you you've always said we're robbers and our business is to rob."

I said, "Well, we're taking a little vacation. That all right?"

He said, "I think we ought to be planning a job. At least talking about one."

Well, this was a complete somersault for both of us and I understood why. Ever since that woman had done it to him, Wilcey had been hot to pull another job. It was like he had nothing left except his profession, and he wanted to be busy with that. That'd been the way of it for me. But now that I had Marianne, I just wasn't in any hellacious rush to risk my neck. Before it hadn't seemed to matter so much. But now, with her, things were damn good, and I didn't much want to take any more chances than I had to.

I said, "We'll pull a job when I get damn good and ready. Now let it alone, Wilcey."

Well, the little flurry between Wilcey and me had kind of dampened my mood. I said, "Let's go up the street and get something to eat. Maybe look around at a few more places. See what's going on."

"Well, all right," Wilcey said. "Though I was kind of thinking of getting into that poker game."

"Let's eat first," I said. "We ain't eat too well the last couple of days on the road from San Antonio."

And in truth, we hadn't. We'd stayed out of the towns and away from the main roads, traveling cross-country and camping out at night and making do with beef and tortillas and some frijoles Chulo's cousin's wife had fixed up for us.

You understand, the border country was my natural range. And even though it was the place I felt the most at home, it was also the place where I'd done the most of my depredations and where I was the most wanted and the most likely to be recognized.

For that reason Wilcey was correct in his apprehensions about us going to Laredo. It was a place I would be likely to be recognized. But it was also a place I understood and it was my country and I knew best how to handle myself in it.

Besides that, I missed it and wanted to go back. True, I wanted to take Marianne to Mexico. She was an Oklahoma girl and she'd never seen my home range, and I felt like she had to if she was to really know me. And I did want her to know me.

We got up. I corked the bottle of brandy and handed it to the barkeep as we passed, telling him to hold it for us, that we'd be back later. We went on out the door and turned in to the blazing heat. The streets, except for a few Mexican peons lolling against the sides of buildings, were pretty well deserted. We walked about a block and then turned in to a place that was about half cafe, half saloon. There was no division between the eating part and the drinking part, but the cafe end had some tables up near windows that faced onto the front, making it lighter in that corner to make it easier, I guessed, to see what you were eating.

We got settled and a fat Mexican woman come over, and we ordered up what they had, tamales and chili con carne and tortillas. She said they had beer, though it wasn't cold. Well, we hadn't expected cold beer so we ordered up some of that and settled down to eat. I was sitting where I could see through this wide archway that looked in to the saloon part of the outfit. There were a half dozen pretty hard-looking cases drinking at the bar. I recognized one of them, though I hadn't ever expected to see him again. It was a man called Austin Davis, a man I'd known down around the Corpus Christi country just as I was coming up as an outlaw. He'd been sort of a ne'er-do-well. Never really in trouble and never really out of it. I reckoned we were close to the same age, and I could see we were still about the same size, six foot and about a hundred and ninety pounds. Last I'd heard of him he'd had to leave the country after killing some woman's husband. I'd heard he'd headed up north, to Montana or some such place. And now here he was back. I could see he still suffered from his old trouble of being just a little too good-looking for his own welfare. But that hadn't protected him none. All I'd ever heard about him was he hadn't had no more luck with women than I had. But there was a difference between us where I was concerned. He had the reputation of a man who'd go after another man's woman. That had never been my style.

I studied him standing there at the bar. He hadn't looked my way, and I doubted if he'd recognize me even if he did. It had been a number of years; maybe twelve or fourteen. I could see he'd become a real hard case. He had his gun well set up on his thigh, and he had the look about him of a man who'd know how to use it if the occasion demanded. I was on the point of mentioning him to my partners when the woman brought our food and we set to the chore of eating.

When we were finished, I lit a cigarillo and leaned back in my chair, smoking and drinking what beer was left in my glass. Davis still hadn't moved. He was at the bar, one foot on the brass rail, looking down at his drink. Down from him two hombres was talking loud at each other, but Davis paid them no mind. I nudged Wilcey and pointed the desperado out to him and told him a little about Davis. Wilcey just shrugged. "Well? So?"

I said, "He's a pretty good man. If we were to be going to pull a job down here, he'd be a good man to have along."

Wilcey said, "But you said we was on vacation. That there wasn't going to be any job."

"All right, Wilcey. But I can't read the future. That's what I'm saying today. Tomorrow it might be different." I give him a disgusted look. "I just thought you'd be interested in who the ol' boy was."

He said, "We going to stay the night here?"

"I don't know," I said. "Do you have to know right now?"

"No, I ain't got to know right now. But I would like to know if we're just going to sit around this hole. I don't see the point to it, but you're the boss."

"Shit, Wilcey," I said. "You wouldn't be happy if you were going to be hung with a new rope." I got up. "Let's go in and have a few drinks. It ought to have cooled off by then, and we'll decide whether to go on or to stay the night."

We started in to the saloon part. Just as we got to the big entranceway that separated the two parts one of the loud-talking hombres at the bar suddenly pushed himself away and started into the cafe. There was plenty of room for him to pass on either side of me, but it seemed as if he just deliberately tried to walk into me. I shoved him back just before we collided, and he stood there staring at me, not saying a word. He was young and looked drunk. I said, "Take it easy, stranger."

We stepped on by him without a word and took a table by the wall and called for a bottle of whiskey. The young man that had almost bumped into me had gone on into the cafe, but he didn't eat. Instead he was back at the bar in about a minute. He stood there, talking to the man on his right and casting little looks at me every now and then.

I figured he was just drunk and feeling his oats. I'd seen his kind about a thousand times before. Sometimes the whiskey made them a little too brave for their own good, and then they had to be dealt with. I generally tried to give them every break I could, but sometimes they'd push too hard and nothing would answer but a quick fight. Most times with fists, but all too often, the guns would have to come out. I watched the young man carefully, hoping this wouldn't be one of those times.

Austin Davis was on the young man's left, but he wasn't paying him any mind, just tending to his drink. The bartender brought us a bottle of bourbon, and we poured out all around and then knocked them straight back for "luck" and then poured out again and sat there sipping our drinks comfortably. I thought the trouble with the young hombre was going to pass, but about then I heard him say to the man on his right, "Yeah? Well, you just watch me!" Then he put his head back, downed a quick shot of whiskey, pushed away from the bar, and came directly to our table. I was sitting with my back to the wall, Wilcey on my left and the black Mexican on my right. We all glanced up as the young man edged up to our table, facing me. He said, "You think you're hot shit, don't you?"

I looked at him a long moment, trying to gauge just how drunk he was. But drunk or not, I wasn't going to take no chances with him. A bullet out of a drunk's gun will kill you just as quick as if you'd been shot by the president of the Women's Christian Temperance Union. I said, carefully, "Well, I never really give it much thought, either way."

"You think you're somethin', don't ya!" he said, slurring his words a little. "Think you can come swellin' 'round here and ever'body's gonna lay down and kiss yore boots. Think I don't know who you are."

I said, "Listen, go on now. I don't want any trouble."

Without seeming to, Chulo pushed his chair out so that he was facing the young man. I sort of shifted myself so that my gun handle came free at my side.

The young man was working himself up. He said, "Think 'cause you're Wilson Young you can scare ever'body. Well, I ain't scairt!" He tapped himself in the chest. "Roy Chester ain't scairt! By God, you get up outten that chair and I'll settle yore hash for you! See if I don't!"

Over his shoulder I saw Davis suddenly push away from the bar and come walking toward us. I didn't know what his intentions were. While we'd never been enemies, we'd never been all that friendly either. I sort of tensed up, getting ready for whatever might come.

I said to the boy, for he looked younger all the time, what with his blustering. I said, "Listen, don't let your mouth get you into more trouble than you can get out of. You're drunk. Now go sleep it off."

But it was Austin Davis that had the majority of my attention. A few feet from the young man, he suddenly pulled his pistol in a smooth gesture. Instinctively my own hand dipped, but he just reversed the gun and with a short, chopping blow caught the young man behind the ear with the butt of his pistol. The man dropped like he'd been pole axed. Then Davis stood there, thoughtfully putting his pistol back in the holster. He said, "Hello, Will. How you been getting along?"

"Howdy, Austin. Doing well, how about yourself?" I stuck out my hand and we shook. I said, "Much obliged for getting me out of that little mess I was about to get in."

Davis grinned slightly and jerked his head toward where the kid lay on the floor. "Likely it's him owes me the thanks. All he got from me was a bump on the head. He'll be glad when he sobers up."

"Well, yes," I said. "He was drunk. But then I been drunk too." I motioned. "Take a chair and have a drink with us."

He said, "Don't mind if I do. Ain't seen you in a good while. Heard plenty about you, though."

Chapter Two

I introduced Davis to my two partners. Austin said, shaking hands with Chulo, "I've heard about this one. Word is he's with you steady now."

"Yes," I said. "Ever'body's got to have a cross to bear. The black Meskin is mine."

Then he and Wilcey shook. Davis didn't have much to say to him. I guess he hadn't heard about Wilcey. We poured out a new round of drinks and then sat there talking. Over Davis' shoulder, I could see the bartender taking the boy by the shoulders and dragging him out the front door. He never even glanced at us. I reckoned he was pretty used to such goings-on.

After a bit Wilcey said, "Will, if we're going to be here awhile, I don't want to just sit around and drink. I think I'll go down to that other saloon and get in that poker game."

"All right," I said. "But take Chulo along with you and get him fucked. He's starting to get nervous."

They left and I watched Wilcey as he went out the door. He was getting mighty edgy since he'd lost that Ruth woman. Hell, I felt sorry for him, but there didn't seem to be a thing I could do or say.

Davis took the bottle and poured our glasses full again. He said, "What you doing in this neck of the woods? Got something planned?"

I shook my head. "No. We're just ambling around, sort of cooling out. Probably heading for Laredo."

Davis said, "I might be going in that direction in a few days. Right now I'm waiting for a man to show up from the south."

"Mexican cattle?"

He nodded. "Yeah. Not very good business, but when that's all you've got you have to make do."

I said, "Been a good while since I've seen you. What, about twelve years? More?"

He shrugged. "About that, I'd reckon. That saloon in Robstown. That time that sheriff recognized you, and you had to make a hasty departure."

He didn't look that much different. Funny thing, time was when people thought we looked something alike, and I reckoned there might have been a slight resemblance. But he was always, I thought, a good deal better-looking than I was, and he was a little lighter, though now, older, he didn't look that much lighter in the face than me. But now he was sporting a handsome handlebar mustache. It made me think I might ought to grow some face whiskers some time, just to make me a little harder to recognize.

I asked him what he'd been up to in those years, and he shrugged and sort of touched the high spots. Said, when he'd run from that trouble here in south

Texas, he'd ended up in Arkansas, but his old women trouble had followed him there, and he'd left one town with a couple of brothers, brothers of a lady who hadn't thought he'd done her right, hot on his trail. After that he'd just kept on drifting north, finally ending up in Montana. He grinned slightly, and said, "Thought I was fixing to get set up in the ranch business, but the old man who was going to fix me up didn't take kindly to me fooling with his young wife so that didn't work out."

I said, "That fooling with another man's woman is going to get you killed one of these days, Austin."

He said, "Oh, I've reformed. Give up that habit."

Which I doubted.

After that, he said he'd stayed up north, more or less hiring out his gun in a lot of the land troubles that were going on up there between the ranchers and the farmers that were settling government claims. He'd been in the Johnson county war and had got shot for his troubles.

He said, "After that I just drifted south, doing whatever would turn a dollar." He looked at me. "You know how that goes."

I nodded. I well knew how that went.

He said, "I've heard considerable about you since I've been back in this part of the country. Sounds like you've been damn busy."

I shrugged. "I'm keeping alive."

He said, "I'm surprised, hot as you are, that you'd be down in this part of Texas. Ain't they going to be looking for you pretty steady?"

"You sound like Wilcey," I said. "Hell, I can't hide all the time." I'd started to tell him that they wouldn't be looking for me with a lady on my arm, but I'd stopped. For some reason I didn't want him to know about Marianne. Not that he'd ever see her, but I just didn't. I guess it was because of his reputation. It didn't make a bit of sense.

He said, "And you ain't got nothing working? Nothing I could have a piece of?"

I shook my head. "No, I don't, Austin. Sorry."

He studied me. "You know I'm a good hand with a gun."

"I ain't doubting that. I'm telling you straight. I ain't got nothing planned."

"Would you keep me in mind if you do? I'm a little short on cash right now."

I promised him his name was in my head if something came up. But I added that I doubted it would.

We sat around talking and visiting a little more, and then I went down to the other saloon and hunted up Wilcey and Chulo. Chulo was in the back with a woman, and Wilcey was playing poker. I'd about made up my mind that there wasn't no reason to get in a rush to go to Laredo, so I told Wilcey I was going down and get us a room at the hotel and I'd probably be there.

We didn't do much the balance of the day except drink some whiskey and eat a little. Wilcey played poker that night, but I just sat in the hotel and did a lot of thinking.

Mostly I thought about Marianne and what we were going to do. She hadn't made any kind of demands on me, and indeed, we'd never really even talked about the future. But I knew we were going to have to pretty soon. In the two months we'd stayed at Chulo's cousin's house, after she recovered from her gunshot wound, we mostly just had a good time and enjoyed each other.

Wasn't any question I loved the woman, and I had every reason to believe that she loved me. But that still didn't change the fact that I was a wanted outlaw and a man with a very uncertain future. If you stopped to think about it, all I could offer Marianne was a life of desperation, of fear, and of being on the run. I couldn't offer her a settled life with a home and security as most women wanted.

So I didn't know where we were going. All I knew was that I wanted her with me the rest of my life. But it damn sure wasn't fair to ask her to accept my kind of life when she could easily do so much better for herself.

I went to sleep that night with the kind of bad feeling that I was going to have to talk to her pretty soon. I figured to give us a few days in Laredo of doing nothing but having a good time, and then I was going to bring it up and see what we could figure out.

When we rode out next morning, Austin Davis was standing on a corner. I returned the little half wave he gave me.

Wilcey said, "You and your friend have a good visit?"

I said, "He ain't exactly a friend. That's the first time I've seen him in about twelve years."

Still I couldn't forget how he'd whopped that yahoo in the back of the head and kept me from maybe doing the killing of a poor drunk young fool that deserved time to think things over.

We had about twenty miles to go to Laredo, which ain't a hard ride if a man is sitting a good horse, and naturally, we were all riding good horses. We did take it in easy stages, however, pulling down to make a noon meal under what shade we could find in that country. After we made a lunch on the beans and biscuits we'd brought from Encinal, I took a bottle of rum and walked a little way from my two partners and shaded up under a pretty poor clump of mesquite trees and sat down to have a little think. Of course, there wasn't much shade in that country, as down-ridden as it was. It was mostly just stunted mesquite trees and rocks and sand and gila monsters and snakes and not much else.

But, like the man said, you done the best with what you had to work with, and they do say that them that ain't used to much can make do with a hell of a lot less than them that are used to more.

And I'd never been used to much.

But I sat there in what little shade I could find and thought. Funny thing was I was thinking about Austin Davis and Marianne. I knew he was a hell of a lady's man, and I got to thinking about what might happen if he ever met Marianne. Not that I ever expected that to happen, but I guess what I was really thinking about was what might happen if she ever met another man that could take my place in her affections. God knows, I knew I wasn't no prize, but the thought of her with another man was like a rusty knife cutting through my belly. I guess it had been in the back of my mind, her with her past, and seeing Austin had just sort of brought it to the forefront of my thinking. I wasn't thinking that he might try and cut into my time with Marianne; he'd know better than that. Because I'd kill, just quicker than a cat could lick its ass, any man that tried to do that. But just thinking what it might feel like to have Marianne with another man bothered me.

Her past I knew all about. But I didn't want to think about it. I wanted to think that I was the first man she'd ever been with, and I wanted to keep it that way in my mind.

A man can do that, you know, when he has to.

But I did sit there and wonder. That goddam Austin was a handsome devil, and I wondered if she loved me enough to be completely hardened to his charms.

Or if she might fall.

For, you see, as hard a case as I was, I loved the woman and jealousy was a strange feeling for me. Oh, I'd thought I'd cared before, but ever since I met Marianne, I'd come to realize that all the past had been nothing but play. With her it had become real, and I'd come to realize and come to worry over the responsibilities of real love.

But what a robber, such as myself, was going to do with real love was a hell of a lot more than I could figure out at that time.

I got up and signaled for us to go on. Chulo and Wilcey mounted at the same time as I did. As we rode off, I looked at them with real affection. I know it might sound a little strange for a man to feel that kind of feeling for two other men, especially two that their own mothers would probably have a hard time loving, but I did. You've got to realize that when you go down the road together, as committed as each of you are to the other, that a special kind of bond develops.

Of course, I wouldn't have dared mention such a thing to either one of them. It would have made all our faces red, and they'd of never forgiven me.

Men don't talk about such things.

But they exist, nevertheless.

The road was plenty hot and dusty. I said, after a time, "Well, we ought to be getting close. Laredo can't be but a few miles farther on up the road."

Chulo said, "Chit, it's hot."

But then he never could say "shit" like a man ought to be able to say. That was the Nigger Meskin for you.

Wilcey said, "What's the name of that hotel Marianne's going to be meeting us at?"

I said, "In the first place she ain't going to be meeting *us*. Once we get into Laredo, we ain't going to be seen together that much. And I believe it's the Palace Hotel."

"Reckon she'll be there?"

I gave him a quick look. "I know damn good and well she'll be there."

We rode on in silence. The road stretched out empty and dusty and straight in front of us. But about a quarter of a mile ahead there was a little clump of stunted oak trees, and even as I looked, I saw three horsemen come out of the trees and ride in our direction. I figured they were just cowboys working on a nearby ranch and didn't think no more of it. And as they got nearer, I could see that they were young and probably of Mexican heritage. I had tensed up a little at the first sight of them, never knowing who might be after me, but then I saw they weren't much more than boys and kind of relaxed. We held to the right side of the road, and they took the opposite, their horses' hooves kicking up little spurts of dust in the bright sunshine. They come on and, just as we met, I started to nod them a greeting. At that instant the two on the outside suddenly pulled pistols, and the one in the middle come up with a shotgun and leveled it down on us. The one with the shotgun said, "Hold it! This is a stickup!"

Well, I was that amazed that, for an instant, I didn't believe it was happening. But there's no running away, especially at such close quarters, from a scatter gun so we immediately stopped our horses.

I just sat my horse, staring at them. I tell you what went through my mind at the instant was something that had happened many years before. It had been my first act of depravation when I was seventeen. I'd been broke and alone with no future and no plans for the future and, in desperation, I'd robbed a rancher and his wife on the road between Calallen and Corpus Christi. The shame that I felt after I'd committed that despicable act had stayed with me through the years. It was the first and last time that I'd ever done robbery on private individuals and certainly private individuals of moderate means. I'd done enough robbing since that time to spend a hundred lifetimes in jail, but from then on I'd only robbed institutions such as banks or trains or huge ranches that were insured and where the person that I was robbing would not be injured.

I know it is hard to understand, from such a robber and outlaw, the shame I later felt for that desperate deed, but it was indeed shame that I felt. I had taken a little over twenty dollars off the rancher and, of that, I believe I'd spent some fifty cents for the first meal I'd eaten in days. And at that, I'd almost had to gag the food down, so bad did I feel. The rest of the money had burned like the coals of hell in my pocket, burned so bad that I'd finally taken it and hid it under a rock, somewhere out on the prairie. Had I been able to have returned the money to the rancher I would have done so, at whatever cost to my own neck it might have meant. But I didn't know his name nor where he lived so all I could do, in the mind of a seventeen-year-old boy, was not profit from my despicable deed any more than the price of that one poor meal I ate.

Yet for many years, the face of that rancher, as I was robbing him and his wife, had haunted me. They had sat there in their buckboard, and he'd very slowly drawn out the worn wallet he had in his hip pocket and turned over the little money he had to me. Probably it was money intended to feed his family or to buy feed for his cattle.

And I had taken it from him.

It had been a low, dishonorable thing to do and I'd never ceased worrying myself about it.

And now, the very same thing was happening to me.

In that instant I realized, more than ever, how helpless that poor rancher had felt. For I had not only robbed him of his money, I had robbed him of his dignity. I had shamed him in front of his wife, and I suppose there were many nights after that that he'd castigated himself because there was nothing that he could do. I had held a drawn gun in my hand, a hand that was shaking next to a trigger that led to a cocked hammer, and that poor honest man had found himself in a situation where there was nothing he could do unless he'd wanted to foolishly risk his life and that of his wife.

For he didn't know me and didn't know that I wouldn't have shot him or his wife. All he saw was a fool kid with a drawn gun. And a nervous kid at that.

Just as what I was looking at. I tell you, there's only one thing that bothers me more than having a gun pointed at me and that is to have the hand that's holding the gun to be shaking.

And all three of them were shaking. There wasn't a one of them who looked to be more than eighteen years old. Chulo and Wilcey were looking at me, and I just sort of slowly shook my head. Then I looked at the one holding the shotgun. I said, "What do you want?"

He said, in a kind of high voice, "We want your money."

I said, just as calm and as quietly as I could, "All right. You tell me how you want me to give it to you and we'll do it. Do you want us to get down or stay mounted? Ain't no reason to worry about anything. We're going to do exactly what you tell us to do."

He said, "Get down off your horses. And be slow about it. This shotgun's got a hair trigger."

I said, "We'll do as you say. Just take it easy. Chulo, you and Wilcey do as the gentleman says."

I was still talking calmly and quietly, but inside, I was beginning to get plenty angry. Hell, I was Wilson Young! And I was being held up by three punk boys with cheap guns.

And there wasn't a damn thing I could do except take it. Or at least take it for the time being.

Also, I was beginning, now that the first reaction had worn off, to get a little worried about the money. I had nearly $6,000 in my saddlebags, and I figured Chulo and Wilcey were carrying about the same amount in theirs. And these boys were planning on robbing it off of us.

Well, I figured it would be a cold day in hell before I let that happen.

We all dismounted and stood there looking at them. I said, "You want us to drop our guns?"

Hell, they were so damn inexperienced I figured they needed some help.

But he said, "Hell, no. You just all three take your money out, just nice and easy, and lay it right there on the ground. And any other valuables you might have."

I said, "The money is in my saddlebags. You want me to untie it and lay it on the ground?"

He had to think about that for a second. Then he said, "Yeah, do that. But you do it careful like. Or I'll shoot you. So help me I will."

The boy was making a lot of mistakes. Especially not taking our guns. He should have made us pitch them out in the brush.

But I stepped to the back of my horse and very carefully untied the saddlebag. I had been riding on the inside, toward the middle of the road, and Wilcey and Chulo were to my right. I gave them a quick glance. They were standing by their horses switching their eyes from me to the three boys. I gave them just the barest of nods to let them know I was fixing to do something and to be ready.

I got the saddlebag untied and drug it off the back of my horse. It was good and heavy, having about a thousand dollars of money in gold in it, which gave it some nice weight.

The boys were about ten feet away, and as I stepped away from my horse, I suddenly threw the saddlebag at the head of the one with the shotgun. In the same instant I dropped to the ground, rolling under my horse and drawing my gun as I came up on the other side. By the flurry of dust, I could tell that Wilcey and Chulo were doing the same. The saddlebag caught the boy flush in the face, knocking him over backward on his horse, his shotgun pointing at the sky and firing harmlessly into the air.

I came up behind my horse, throwing my gun arm across my saddle and leveling down on the three. "Hold it!" I yelled. "Goddammit: DROP THOSE GODDAM GUNS!"

Well, the two on the outside were so startled they didn't move for a second. It had all happened so fast, and they were so inexperienced that they'd been caught completely off guard, and now it was they who were looking at three drawn guns. The one with the shotgun was still on the ground, his scatter gun having bounced a few feet from him. I yelled, "You on the ground! Stay there or I'll kill you!"

He dropped flat. The other two had let go their pistols and were staring in slack-faced surprise at us. I imagine they were surprised. All of a sudden they weren't the big shots they'd seen themselves as, but just scared little boys. I said, "Now you two get off your horses! Move, dammit!"

When they had dismounted, I came around my horse and said, "Wilcey, you get their guns. Chulo, line those little babies up over there by the side of the road."

Chulo said, "We keel them?"

"Not yet," I said. "Not unless they try to run."

Then I turned around and walked back down the road. I was so damn mad I nearly couldn't see straight, and I knew that if I got near them before I cooled down

I'd probably break their necks. In fact I was a little surprised I hadn't killed them when I'd thrown the saddlebag and had a gun on them. But it's always been my style to never kill nobody that ain't got a chance against me or except when they don't give me no selection.

I finally stopped a little way up the road and turned around and stared back. Chulo had the three boys lined up on the side of the road, just as I'd told him, and he and Wilcey were just standing there waiting for me to get back. Well, I still didn't know what I was going to do to them, but I did know they weren't going to get off scot-free. I walked back, studying them as I came. I could tell they were poor from their clothes and the quality of their weapons and the condition of their horses, but, hell, I didn't consider that no excuse.

And I wasn't interested in being no do-gooder and hoping to keep them from following in my footsteps. I knew that wouldn't do no good in the first place and, in the second place, I didn't give a damn.

No, I was interested in making sure they never tried nothing so foolish again as trying to rob me. For, next time, I might have to kill them and that would do a harm to me.

Chulo turned, grinning, his big, white teeth flashing in his black face. "You want Chulo keel them now?"

I said, "No, I don't want Chulo *keel* them now." I was still angry as hell and in no especial mood to put up with his humor. I walked straight up to the one who'd held the shotgun. He was on the end nearest to me. As I come up I could see them kind of falling back a little. They didn't look so brave now; just a bunch of scared boys. I walked straight up to the first one and slapped him, hard and stinging, a fore slap and then a back hand. His head snapped back and forth, and a little blood suddenly jumped out from the corner of his mouth. Then I slapped the next one the same way and then the third one.

They were not Mexicans as I'd first thought, but Texans. They were small and dark from being out in the sun was what had first made me think that.

I stepped back and stared at them. Now they were really looking scared. I said, "You goddam little bastards, I ought to kill all three of you! Goddam you to hell, throwing down on me! Do you know who you just tried to rob? You got any idea? Goddammit," I said to the one with the shotgun. "Speak up! Answer me!"

They were all kind of hanging their heads, looking mighty worried. I said, "I ASKED YOU A QUESTION!"

The one on the end said, "Please, mister, let us go. We be mighty sorry. We won't do it again."

I said, "You goddam right you won't rob me again. Or you won't try and rob me. Next time you do I'll kill all three of you. I asked you, do you little fools know who you just tried to rob?"

Behind me, Wilcey said, warningly, "Will!"

But I ignored him. I asked the fool kids again and finally the one in the middle said, "No sir. No sir."

I said, "Well, you just tried to rob Wilson Young."

They'd been standing there hanging their heads, but when I said my name, they all come up with startled looks on their faces. I said, "Yeah, that's just what big goddam fools you are. Shit! You little bastards couldn't rob the coins out of your mother's egg money. Tried to rob three desperate outlaws! You little bastards don't know shit!" I was really starting to work myself up. Then I felt a hand on my arm. It was Wilcey. He said, "Take it easy, Will."

I glanced around at him. He said, "You're getting too damn mad."

"Yeah," I said. I heaved a deep breath and started to calm down a little. The three boys were staring at me with fear deep in their eyes. I said, "Yeah, I ought to either kill them or turn them loose."

The one in the middle immediately said, "Oh, gawd, mister, don't kill us! My mother—"

I said, "Don't hand me that shit about your mother. You probably ain't even got a mother. And if you do, she ain't going to have a son much longer you little bastards keep trying to be road agents." I stepped back and pointed up the road away from Laredo. "All right, get to walking. Or better yet, get to running."

They looked a minute like they didn't believe me. Then they started to move toward their horses. I booted the one nearest in the ass and said, "No horses! Get on shank's mare and get to running!"

Well, they had the good sense to realize they'd better git while the gitting was good. I called after them, "And don't look back or slow down! I'll be watching."

Within ten yards they were trotting, and then they were breaking into a run, kicking up little spurts of dust as they did. I turned to Wilcey. He was holding the guns he'd collected from the boys. "Break up those guns, Wilcey. And you, Chulo, unsaddle and unbridle those horses and turn them loose."

I walked over to Wilcey's saddlebags and jerked out a bottle of rum, pulling the cork out with my teeth. It had got plenty hot in the sun and the fumes rising out of the bottle nearly took my head off. But I gagged down a drink of the warm stuff and let it settle. I was still plenty angry, thinking about the close place three goddam kids had almost put us in. I took another drink of the rum, feeling it burn all the way down, and commenced to settle down a little. Wilcey had finished breaking up the boy's guns on a handy rock, and he threw the pieces out into the brush and then come over and took the bottle of rum from me and had a pull.

"Damn!" he said, jerking the bottle away from his mouth. "That stuff's near boiling."

I said, "It's hot enough of itself without no help from the sun."

He had another pull and then handed me the bottle back. I stood there just leaning up against his horse, watching those boys hot footing it on down the road.

Wilcey said, "I don't reckon I ever seen you that mad. Hell, they was just kids."

I said, "That was the point." I took another pull out of the rum and said, "Wilcey, I never felt so goddam helpless in all my life. It makes a body think. You know, I've often thought about the desperate life we lead, with every man's hand against us, and how dangerous it is. But just think—what if we'd of just been three ordinary citizens and not the gunmen that we are and as used to them kind of situations as we are. We'd for sure of been robbed and maybe, if we'd lost our heads and done something foolish, would of been killed."

Wilcey took the bottle back, took a drink, and then shook his head. "That's a hell of a way of looking at it, Will. But then you always was of a strange turn of mind."

I kind of half laughed. "I was just thinking. All the robberies I've pulled. And here I nearly got held up myself by three goddam snot-nosed kids who didn't have sense enough to even pull a proper robbery. Why, it's goddam insulting!" I laughed again. "You know what I was thinking at one point? I was thinking of all the guns I've faced and all the shots I've had shot at me by men who knew what they were doing, and I said, well, goddam, after all this time I'm fixing to get killed by a little boy holding a cheap goddam shotgun. Wasn't even a good piece! I tell you, it embarrasses me."

Wilcey said, "I reckon that's what made you so angry. The insult of the matter."

"Yeah," I said. "Just about! I kept wanting to tell that snot-nosed kid with the shotgun when he was ordering me what to do, I kept wanting to say, you damn little fool. I'm Wilson Young and this is my gang! You can't hold us up!"

Chulo came up just then, having slapped the kids' horses into a run across the prairie. I pitched him the bottle and he took a drink, watching me and Wilcey laugh.

"What the choke?" he asked.

I shoved away from Wilcey's horse. "Ain't no *choke*, Nigger," I said. "Let's mount up and ride for Laredo."

As we rode away I looked back over my shoulder, but the three little boys were now out of sight. I still

THE TEXAS BANK ROBBING COMPANY

couldn't help thinking, however, how all of my victims must have felt.

But at least my hand wasn't shaking. At least when they got robbed by me they got robbed by an expert. And I never shot nobody by accident or out of nervousness. But it was still funny to speculate on what the outcome of that attempted robbery would have been if I had been successful in leading a straight honest life.

Probably I'd of been killed. Robbed for sure. It made me laugh again. But all's well that ends well.

Wilcey said, "Will, I don't think you should have told them your name."

He had that worried sound in his voice again. I said, "Aw, don't start playing the old woman again. I swear, Wilcey, you worry more than any grown man I know."

"Nevertheless," he said, "I don't think you ought to have told them boys who you are. They was coming from Laredo, and they might get back there while we're still there."

I was riding in the middle. I looked over at him. "And so what if they do? You reckon they going to *tell* on me? Hell, I doubt if they want much to do with the law right now."

"I just don't know why you did it. It just didn't sound like you."

"I was mad," I said. "Dammit! And I'm fixing to get mad again if you don't shut up about it."

But naturally, he wouldn't let it alone. He never would. He said, "Well, I still don't think we ought to be going to Laredo. And you doing something like that only makes it worse."

I swung around in my saddle. "Where would you like

us to be going? Do you know a real safe place we can go? If you do, just speak up. Just tell me and we'll by God point the horses in that direction."

"But Laredo," he said. "My God! Where you've committed God knows how many depredations."

"And where there's less law," I reminded him. "And where I got more friends. You're worried about those boys recognizing me after I told them my name. Hell, I bet they's a thousand people in Laredo know who I am. It's as good a place to go as any. Don't you remember? When we were in Houston you wanted to go to the border. Now that we're going to the border you want to go the other way. I swear, one of these days you are going to aggravate me to the point of violence!"

He said, "We're just going to Laredo because Marianne's never been there."

I said, sharply, "Now that, by God, is enough, Wilcey. You shut that kind of talk up."

And as always, when he seen I meant it, he would let something lie. But I'll tell you, it seemed as if he'd been getting more and more worrisome ever since that woman Ruth had turned on him in Houston. I guess it really hurts a man, who'd quit trusting as long as Wilcey had, only to trust again and reap the fruit of another treachery as a result. Like I say, he'd always had a little of the old woman in him, but now it seemed as if he worried over everything. Well, I guess I couldn't really blame him, not after the cards that bitch had dealt him.

I knew he made those remarks about Marianne because it hurt him to see us so happy. Not that he was jealous of my good fortune or wanted to see me have as bad luck as he had had; no, Wilcey ain't that way.

I knew that it was just a reminder to him of what he'd lost, and he couldn't help showing his pain.

But we went on down the road in good style. Me in a rapidly improving mood as I looked forward to seeing Marianne again after our short separation.

Chapter Three

I went into the Palace Hotel with just the slightest worry. We had agreed that Marianne would register under the last name of May. Her real last name was Mason, but we'd thought it better to cover as many tracks as we could. I knew I had no reason to worry about her being there if it was within her power, but I tell you, there's many a slip betwixt the cup and the lip and more things that can go wrong than can be imagined by the mind of such a man as I.

So it was with considerable relief that the clerk told me she was registered and, as far as he knew, was in her room.

You understand it was no big thing, in such a town and in such a hotel as the Palace, for a man to go up to a lady's room. Laredo was the kind of town where you minded your own business or you regretted it— and sometimes in very short order. Which was a situation that Wilcey didn't quite understand else he

THE TEXAS BANK ROBBING COMPANY

wouldn't have worried so much. It was also the case that had caused me to select Laredo as our next hideout when I had begun to think that San Antonio was about to become too warm for our presence.

She was on the second floor, and I ran up the stairs in great anticipation. I knocked at her door and she opened almost immediately. God, she looked as good and as beautiful as she had when I'd left her four days before in San Antonio. We hugged and kissed and then we went and sat down on the bed and she said, "You're a day late. Where have you been? Have you been misbehaving?"

"Never, my darling," I said, kissing her. "Not since I met you." I went ahead and told her that we'd got tired and fell off the road and spent the night in Encinal. I said, "But Chulo misbehaved in Encinal. I think he misbehaved with every girl in town."

She said, "Chulo always misbehaves."

God, she looked pretty; soft and blonde and white and just a little plump. I didn't know for sure, because I'd only been with her in the spring and early summer, but I had the feeling that plump would feel mighty good next to a man on a cold winter's night.

She was wearing a blue gown that revealed just the top of her breasts. I leaned down and kissed her soft skin where they joined.

"No you don't, mister," she said. "Not until you've had a bath. You smell like a goat."

I rolled off the bed and lit a cigarillo. Good girl that she was she had a bottle of good brandy and a pitcher of water sitting on the bedside stand. I poured us out both a glass, put more water in hers than mine, and we said, "Luck" and then knocked them straight back as befits the toast. She'd learned that from being around me, for it was an outlaw's toast and if there's anyone needs luck more than an outlaw I'd reckon it'd be a preacher trying to gather up alms for the poor at a convention of bankers.

I poured out another and then walked over to the window to survey the scene. As I'd told her she'd got us a room that fronted on the street. I raised the window and leaned out, noting with satisfaction that there was the sloping roof of a porch just below. If a man had to he could go out the window, slide down the porch roof, and then have a not too bad a jump down to the street. It was watching little things like that that had kept me out of jail for so long. But of course, I wasn't ever going to jail. They might kill me as, indeed, they might, but they wasn't ever going to lock me up. I'd come to that conclusion a long time ago, that I'd much rather be dead than confined.

I said, "I ain't had nothing to eat. How about you?"

She said, "I been waiting for you. There's a good cafe right next door."

I said, "How's it if we go eat now? I'll book a bath at the desk on the way out and then get cleaned up when we get back."

Well, as it turned out you didn't have to book a bath anymore and have a string of boys bringing in buckets of water. Now they had a tank right there in the bathroom and you could take a bath whenever you wanted. Of course, it wasn't nothing new to me. The hotel that Marianne and I had stayed at in Houston had a bathroom on every floor. No, the only reason I was surprised was that progress was catching up to Laredo.

Something I thought would never happen. But apparently, the times they were a-changing.

We had a pretty good meal at the cafe next door, eating enchiladas and chili and salad and melon. They even had cold beer. I tell you it had been several years since I'd been in Laredo, but there was even some changes going on I couldn't have forecast.

After we'd eaten I sat there drinking beer and looking at Marianne, watching her drink a cup of coffee.

She kind of half blushed, which wasn't hard to see on her fair face. She said, "Quit staring at me. What's the matter with you, cowboy? Ain't you got no manners?"

I said, "It ain't that you're so pretty, lady, it's just that I been looking at Chulo for the last four days and my eyes are hurting so bad I thought to rest them on you."

She made a face at me and I said, "Well, what do you want to do first? Go over to Mexico?"

She gave me a startled look. "You mean we ain't in Mexico already?"

I didn't know if she was kidding or not. Finally, I decided she wasn't. I guess if you didn't know better you couldn't tell Laredo from Nuevo Laredo, which is in Mexico. However, there is a river in between. I said, "You did say you was from Oklahoma? You sure it wasn't someplace a little farther north?"

"Whatever do you mean?"

"We're still in Texas, darlin'. There's the matter of the Rio Grande you have to cross before you're in Mexico."

"Oh," she said and had the good grace to blush.

GILES TIPPETTE

I called for our score and while I waited for it to come asked if she'd felt all right while waiting for me.

"What do you mean?"

"Oh, just you here by yourself those two days. I wondered if you'd been afeared."

She gave me a look. "Cowboy, how long do you think I've been on my own? You think this is my first time in a strange town by myself?"

Well, I'd forgotten. And now it was my turn to feel silly. I said, "Well, what I guess I meant was how scared was I for you to be here two days by yourself. You may be used to it, but I ain't used to having my woman alone in a strange town for two days."

She looked at me curiously. "You're a strange man, Wilson Young. Not at all what one would think."

I said, "Let's go back to the hotel and let me take a bath." I paid the bill and we got up and sauntered out the door and turned left toward the half block to the hotel. But what was my shock when we were nearly to the door but to see Austin Davis tying his horse in front and mounting the sidewalk as if to enter the hotel. He hadn't seen us and I thought he might not, but then he turned his head our way and stopped as we came walking up. There was no way to avoid him. We met right in front of the hotel door. He said, "Why, hello, Will. Didn't know you was headin' for Laredo."

"Yeah," I said.

"Wish you'd of mentioned it. I'd of rode in with ya'll. I guess I got off not much more than two 'er three hours after you and yore partners."

He was talking to me, but he was looking at Marianne, and she was looking at him. I didn't like it, didn't like it at all.

Austin said, "Ain't you gonna introduce me to the little lady, Will?"

"Yeah," I said, not happy about it. "This is Marianne. Marianne, this is Austin."

The sonofabitch took off his hat and swept it before her in a little bow. "My deep pleasure, ma'am. Austin Davis is now your servant."

The sonofabitch had had to tell her his whole name. I said, "She's already got one, Austin. This is my wife."

He give me a kind of surprised look. At my side I kind of felt Marianne was doing the same. He said, "Well, hell, Will. I never knew you were married. And a mighty pretty bride, I must say. I give you compliments."

"Thanks," I said. "Well, we got to go in. I need a bath."

"I was fixing to get a room here myself," he said.

Which had been what I was afraid of. But there wasn't much I could say. I kind of wheeled Marianne through the door and over to the stairs. Just as we took the first step I looked back to see Austin leaning an elbow at the desk and staring after us, or after Marianne. And then I glanced at her and she was looking at Davis. I tell you it give me a bad feeling, but I didn't say anything.

We went to the room and I told Marianne to get me a change of clothes out of her bag. She'd brought with her the new clothes I'd bought in San Antonio, they being sure to receive better care that way than in my saddlebags.

She said, "Why did you tell that man I was your wife?"

I said, "I don't know. Just seemed the right thing to say at the time."

"Well, I don't understand that. Who was that, anyway?"

"Who?" My mood was getting blacker and blacker.

"That man downstairs."

"Just a man I've known. Another outlaw."

She still didn't know how I was feeling. She said, "God, he certainly is good-looking. I bet he's broke many a heart. And such beautiful manners. Did you see how he swept his hat off?"

I said, "Get my goddam clothes, will you! Goddammit!"

She'd been bending over her suitcase, which was laying on the bed. Now she turned around with a startled look. "Why, whatever! What's the matter with you?"

"Nothing," I said. I went to the bedside table and poured myself a hooker of brandy and downed it. "Nothing. Just get my clothes."

But she was standing there studying me. "What's the matter, Will?"

I made a kind of effort to get a handle on my jealousy. I had no reason for it. I guess I'd just been building things up in my mind. I said, "I guess I'm just hot and tired and dirty and need a bath. I'll feel better in a little."

She let it go at that, but she was watching me as I went out of the room and down to the bathroom. It was empty and I got inside and run the tub full out of the overhead tank they had there. Then I took off my clothes, laid them on a little stool, put my gun on top, then put my hat over my gun, pulled the little stool up next to the tub, and climbed inside. The warm water felt mighty good on my old tired hide, and normally, I would have taken great pleasure from such a bath, but I couldn't get my mind off Austin Davis and Marianne. I knew there was no reason to be harboring such dark thoughts, knew I was being a jackass, but sometimes a man's mind will just run away with him.

I didn't stay in the bath long, didn't even take time to enjoy it. I just got out after I soaped and rinsed and dried off and put on my clean clothes. I did take time, before I pulled on my boots, to sit on the little stool and light a cigarillo and think just a bit. Was I, I asked myself, so unsure of Marianne that I feared she'd immediately throw me over for someone such as Austin because he was a good-looking man? Was I then proposing to never trust her? To fear every time she looked at another man?

Was I, really, not going to be able to forget her past? Just because Austin Davis had the reputation of being a lady killer was I going to believe that Marianne would be no different, that she too would succumb to his charms? And if I was going to think like that, how was I ever going to hope that we could make anything important out of the beginning we'd made?

Well, I'm a pretty smart man, but even to a dumb man, the answers to all the questions I was asking myself were no. No, I couldn't mistrust her, and, no, I couldn't believe she'd fall for anyone and throw me over. The only question I could answer yes to was if I would be able to forget her past as a prostitute. I had to answer yes to that one or throw my saddle on my horse and leave town.

But, still, it just made me angry as hell seeing Austin Davis starting his courtly manners on Marianne. It made me so goddam mad I flung my cigarillo onto the floor and stomped at it with my bare foot. That sonofabitch! He ever flirted with her again and I'd, by God, kill him!

And no mistake.

I pulled on my boots, jammed on my hat, and, carrying my gun belt in my hand, went back down to the room. I got inside, jammed a chair up under the knob like I always done, then hung my gun belt over the back of a chair. Marianne had changed. She was wearing nothing but the clinging, blue silk gown she knew I liked so well. She was laying on the bed, watching me.

She said, "You in a better mood now?"

"Yeah," I said, but there was still a little growl in my voice. I walked over to the table and poured myself a glass of straight brandy, then went and sat on the side of the bed. Marianne raised up until she was leaning against my back and put her arms around me. She said, "You still didn't shave."

I didn't say anything. My mood was black. And it didn't seem as if I could do anything about it, no matter how hard I talked to myself.

Marianne reached up and began kissing me on the back of the neck and around the ears. I didn't do anything, just sipped at my drink. She suddenly stopped and I felt her pull back. She said, "Say, what the hell's the matter with you?"

I got up. I had to go and handle this matter. I had

54

to get it out of my mind for it was me that had put it in there. I walked across the room and started strapping on my gun belt. Marianne was watching me in amazement. She said, "Wilson Young, what the hell's the matter with you! Where do you think you're going?"

I said, "I've got some business to attend to, Marianne."

"Now? You mean, right now! You're going out now?"

"Yes," I said.

In a flat voice she said, "I don't believe I ever been so goddam insulted in all of my life."

Well, it was making me feel bad. It was no way to be treating a good woman like Marianne and the fault was all mine. There was no way I could tell her about it. I was too ashamed. I went over and sat down on the edge of the bed. But I couldn't even quite look at her. All I could see in my mind's eye was the look Austin Davis had given her and the way he'd swept his hat off.

I said, "Honey, I'm sorry. This can't wait. It's got to do with Wilcey and Chulo. I've got to get them lined out or it could be trouble."

"Oh," she said, a little uncertainly. "I see. Is it bad?"

"It could get bad," I said. "If I don't tend to it right now. If I let it go on without tending to it, it could get real bad." I turned around and kissed her lightly on the lips. "Besides," I said, "until I get this off my mind I wouldn't be no good to you or to me."

That last part, at least, had been true.

Then she very sweetly reached up and kissed me on the cheek. "I understand, honey," she said.

Which made me feel more like a jackass than ever. But a man has to do what he has to do. Especially a man like me. I very often go straight ahead, even when I'm not right.

She said, as I got up, "Will you be long?"

I shook my head. "I don't think so. But you stay right here in the room. I'll hurry all I can."

I went downstairs without the faintest idea of what I was going to do. In the lobby I stopped and looked around. It was just a little lobby with a few of those straight-backed Mexican chairs scattered around. Wasn't anybody there except the desk clerk. There was a little bar through one door, and I went and looked in there, but it too was empty. It was the siesta hour, a custom observed on the Texas side as much as on the Mexican.

Well, I stood there and thought. I couldn't very well go over and ask what room Austin Davis was registered in, for I knew damn good and well that he wasn't registered under his own name. He might use bad judgment about which ladies he flirted with, but I knew he wasn't no damn fool.

I went out on the street and walked up about a block and looked in one saloon that I found there. They were doing some business, but Davis wasn't among the patrons. Then I walked across the street and checked another. He wasn't in that one either. Finally, I went on back to the hotel, thinking that if I described Austin to the desk clerk he might tell me what room he was in. But I doubted that. Room clerks in Laredo got better sense than that. Especially anything involving a *pistolero*-looking sonofabitch like Austin.

I got in the lobby and was about to go over to the

desk, when I saw a door open down a little hall that led off the first floor of the hotel. It was Austin. He paused a minute to shut his door and then turned toward the lobby. I walked toward him rapidly so as to intercept him in the hall. He saw me coming and stopped. "Why, hello, Will," he said as I came up. "Was about to look you up. By the way, congratulations on your wife. A mighty pretty lady."

I said, "That's what I wanted to talk to you about."

I walked on by him, there in the hall, halting after a few steps. I felt him coming up behind me, and I suddenly whirled, grabbed him by the shirt front with my left hand, dropped my right hand to the butt of my revolver, and slammed him up against the wall. I slammed him hard enough that it kind of made him "Oooof." I had my left elbow pressed up against his right arm so that he couldn't have drawn very well, and I was standing close enough to him that he'd of had a hard time getting off a shot. He didn't resist, just had a surprised look on his face.

I said, lowly and flatly, "Listen, you sonofabitch, I know your reputation with the ladies. You looked at my wife a little over-long this morning. You ever look at her again, you ever touch her, you even say anything other than good morning to her and I'll blow you to Kingdom Come!"

He just stared back at me, though the surprise had turned to something like bewilderment. I jerked him out a little and then slammed him back against the wall again. "You understand me, Davis! Do you understand me!"

His face got calm. I'll hand him that. He was a cool customer, all right. I said, again, "Do you understand me? I'll put a hole through you God didn't intend for you to have."

He said, "I hear your words."

I looked him in the eyes a long second, letting him know that I meant what I said. Then I stepped slowly back, watching his gun hand. But he just kind of relaxed up against the wall, reaching up one hand to straighten his collar. I took two steps backward, still watching him, but he made no move to make a play. I turned on my heel. He wasn't a man to shoot you in the back. He might take your woman, but he wasn't a bushwhacker.

I had taken a couple of steps, when I heard him say, "Young."

I turned, wondering if he was going to make a play. But he was still just standing there by the wall. He said, "I want you to know I won't ever take that again. I know I probably ain't no match for you, but if you ever pull that on me again, I'm going to have to try."

I didn't say anything, just stared at him.

He said, "I know what my reputation is about women and even about some other men's wives. But you don't know enough about me to know that I never did it to a friend. And I ain't going to start. And I considered you a friend."

I said, "You gave her a goddam good looking over."

He said, "You damn right I did. She's a damn good-looking woman and any man in his right mind is going to give her a good looking over."

I didn't say anything, just let his words go around in my head.

He said, "I ain't going to hold this against you or be looking to get back at you, for I know what love feels like and how it can make you act. But I've already told you I won't be shamed again like you just done me. Even if I get kilt for it."

I said, "I wasn't shaming you. I was warning you."

"I didn't need no warning. Once I understood she was your wife I'd of never looked at her again."

"Or my woman," I said.

"Wife, woman. It's the same thing."

Well, I didn't know what to think.

He said, "I'll tell you one more thing, too, Will. You ain't ever going to stop men from looking at a woman that good-looking. You go to killing every man that looks at her and there won't be a man left alive on the streets." He came toward me, and as he passed he said, "You ought to be proud of it."

Then he went through the lobby and on out the front door. I stood staring after him, not quite sure what to think. After a moment I went on back upstairs. I wasn't sure if I'd been right, but I was glad I'd done it. I was feeling a lot easier in my mind. I knew there were folks wouldn't ever understood how I thought, but they'd have to be me to be able to do that, and instead of judging me, they ought to just thank their lucky stars they weren't me.

When I got in the room Marianne was laying on her back on the bed, propped up on a couple of pillows. Her robe had come open in front, exposing her white, plump breasts and her little stomach and that little, soft growth of blond hair where her legs joined. I got my clothes off as fast as I could and crawled in and just kind of smothered myself in her. Just became a part of her and felt all her warmth and softness, felt those arms around my neck, felt her smooth skin against mine, felt all that tenderness coming from her that nobody had ever given me before.

I guess I figured it out then. Why I'd acted so about her. She was the first thing of worth I'd ever been given. Everything else I'd ever gotten I'd had to rob for it. Nobody had never given me nothing.

Not until her. And she'd given me herself. I guess I still couldn't believe my good fortune.

Not after all the long, hard years.

Sometime later we got up and dressed. While she was getting herself together I went down and, as she said, shaved just a little too late.

Walking down the stairs, she asked me, "What's Mexico like?"

I said, "Well, it's dirty and mean and dangerous and full of people who don't give a damn if they live or die. It's also about as good a place as I know outside of Texas. Which don't say a hell of a lot for Texas, does it?"

Our hotel wasn't but a few blocks from the bridge, but I elected to halt one of those open carriages and give her the grand tour of the place. I helped her in and gave the driver a gold peso and told him to just drive wherever I directed.

It was a nice night, with a good moon and just enough coolness in the air to make you appreciate the heat of the day. We drove across the bridge, stopped just briefly by the Mexican Customs who were about half asleep, even at that early hour.

She had chosen to wear a white gown that clasped at the throat with some sort of blue jewelry geegaw that pretty well set off her looks. I sat by her in the carriage holding her hand like some kind of goddam schoolboy. The driver, as some of them Mexicans will do, had put some sort of silly cockade on his horse's head to sort of dress up the rig. Never mind the poor goddam horse's ribs are showing for lack of feed; they'll do something silly like put a half-dyed broom on his head and hope no one notices that the damn horse is about to die.

But that was Mexico for you. We got into the main part of Nuevo Laredo, heading toward the main plaza, and Marianne kind of sat up and said, "Now I'm in a foreign country. I never been in a foreign country before."

Well, that struck me as kind of funny. I guess it hit me that way because I'd never considered the border country, on either side of the river, as foreign. I said to her, still kind of laughing, "Well, I don't know about that. I always thought I was in a foreign country anytime I got over a hundred miles north of the border country."

Because the border country had always been my home and I guess that was what had drawn me back there with her, I guess I wanted to show Marianne where I lived.

We found the main plaza and I bade the driver to stop and wait and we got out and went and sat down on one of the benches. The moon was up full and the plaza, under whatever kind of trees lined it, was shaded in the middle. There was a few other people there, a couple walking here and there, but mainly we had it to ourselves. We sat down on one of the concrete benches that was around the outside, and I lit a cigarillo and put my arm around Marianne. Behind us the carriage waited at the curb.

She said, "So, I'm in Mexico."

"Yeah."

She said, "And you've been here before?"

I didn't say anything for a minute. Ever since we'd come rumbling across the bridge in the carriage, a strong feeling had been coming over me. How long had it been since I'd been in Nuevo Laredo? Six, eight years? Something like that. More like eight. I'd split up with Les Richter to go to Sabinas Hidalgo to try and court that little high-born *señorita* that I'd never had a chance with. And then had come the telegram for me from Black Jack, an old friend of ours, saying Les was near dying in the Nuevo Laredo Infirmary.

And I'd almost killed a good horse rushing up from Sabinas Hidalgo to rescue him. He'd been shot by two bounty hunters, Bill Morton and Bob Bird, who'd followed us across the border after that mess of a bank robbery we'd tried to pull in Uvalde, Texas. I'd got there just in time to find he was already dead, but still laying there in that infirmary. I'd gone there and Morton had been guarding the front door with a shotgun, just waiting to see who'd come along. He'd been waiting for me, only he didn't know it was me. I'd killed him before he could get that shotgun up, making sure he knew who it was shot him before he'd died.

I'd felt no sorrow, for I'd found out how they'd killed Les. They'd surprised him in his hotel room and shot him five times without giving him a chance to say anything.

Of course, he'd died. He'd been dead before they'd ever taken him to that infirmary to use as bait.

So my heart had been very hard when I'd gone to the very same hotel to seek out Bob Bird after I'd killed Morton. I'd caught him in bed in his room and I'd faced him with a drawn revolver. He'd whined; he'd said that it wasn't my style to kill an unarmed man. I'd reminded him of how they'd shot Les. I'd let him talk too long and he'd snaked his hand out and thrown a little table at me that had given him time to come out from under the pillow with a hideout gun. He'd managed to shoot me twice before I could kill him. After that I'd staggered out of the hotel, somehow finding my way down by the railroad tracks, hoping, I supposed, to find a train out of there before the law found me. Then I'd passed out. Next I'd remembered had been two little old Mexican ladies trying to nurse me back to health. They'd found me and drug me into their hovel and kept me alive, God knows how, until my strength had come back. I'd given them, when I left, what little money I had left, but I'd always hoped to find those guardian angels again and thank them properly, but the opportunity had never come about. Now, I reckoned, it had passed for all time.

But sitting there on that bench, all those feelings came flooding back over me. All those memories. It made me forget the night and the moon and the peace of that plaza and that I was with the woman I loved. It made me remember the boom of the guns in Bird's room, the smoke, Les' death, the feeling that I was dead, those long weeks to get myself back together. All that came back to me in that moment sitting there, and I could not just enjoy where I was and what I was doing. I had to go revisit the past.

Maybe Wilcey had been right. Maybe I shouldn't have come back to Laredo. Except he didn't know why I shouldn't have come back.

I suddenly grabbed Marianne's hand and jerked her up and said, "Let's go to the carriage. I want to ride. I want to show you some things."

We went back and got in and I conversed rapidly with the driver in Spanish. He gave me a kind of surprised look, but then he nodded and slapped his horse with the reins and we set off toward another part of town.

Marianne said, "Where are we going?"

I said, "Shut up. I want to show you some places."

She said, "What?"

She sounded bewildered, but I didn't give a damn. My mood was what it was, and she could take it or leave it. She hadn't come to Nuevo Laredo the last time with her best friend killed.

I had.

And I made no apologies for the way I felt. Nor was I going to do much explaining.

We drove first to the little infirmary where Les had been wrapped in a shroud and laid on a bed. I'd never gotten inside. Morton had been waiting by the front door with a shotgun. I'd come up to him, asked him for a light for the cigarillo I'd had hanging out of my mouth, and the fool had wasted the half second he had left to live reaching in his pocket for a lucifer match. Then, as I'd been stepping back, he'd said, "Who—"

Only he'd never got any further. I'd pulled and shot him in the belly, the chest, and then in the neck as he'd been going over backward. I'd said, just before I'd shot him, "Wilson Young. And here's yours."

When we pulled up in front of the infirmary, the driver looked back at me like he wasn't sure that was where I'd directed him. But I nodded and got out.

THE TEXAS BANK ROBBING COMPANY

Marianne said, "Will, where the hell is this?"

I just said, "Get down."

Then I stood there looking at the front of that little whitewashed building, remembering that night again.

It didn't look much different. Just a little adobe, low-roofed building that held people either trying to get better or to die. The front steps where I'd killed Morton were still there.

I stood there, in the moonlight, remembering it.

She said, "Why are we here? What is this place?"

I said, "You've heard me speak of the best friend a man ever had. Les Richter. This is where he died. After two bounty hunters bushwhacked him." I pointed toward the front steps. "There is where I killed one of them. Now let's get back in the carriage. I want to show you another place."

I had another conversation with the driver and then we set off again. Marianne was sitting next to me, close, and I could feel her looking at me. But I kept staring straight ahead. She said, "Will, what are you doing?"

"Nothing," I said. Then I realized that wasn't the truth. So I said, "Telling you about me."

"But I already know you."

I turned and looked at her. I said, "No, you don't. You just think you do. You better see some of the things that cause me to act like I do sometimes. Then maybe you'll understand better who you're getting involved with."

"All right," she said. She put both her hands to my arm and cupped them around it.

We went back to the main part of the town and pulled up in front of the hotel that was just a little ways off the plaza. I got out and helped her down and then bade the driver wait. We went inside and, without a word, I led her up the stairs to the second floor and then down the hall and stopped opposite a door I remembered only too well.

I gestured and said, "Inside that door, in that room, was one of the two men who killed my partner. The last time I was here I kicked it in and went in there and killed him. Except he wounded me twice before I got the deed done. You've asked me about the bullet scars on my body." I touched just under my collar bone and my side. "Those were two that I got right here."

She looked up at me, seeing, I reckoned, the pain on my face. She said, "Will, you don't have to."

I said, "Yes, I do. I come out that door, that door right there, badly wounded. And I walked down the stairs and out the front door. Come on. I'll show you where I went."

We went back downstairs and got in the carriage, and I gave the driver directions. It was strange wandering through that little distance in a carriage, going past the trees and darkness and the silent houses that I'd staggered past in that distant night so long ago. We came to the train depot and I had the driver stop and then we got down and started walking up the tracks. We walked perhaps a hundred yards, walked to where a ditch began on the side of the tracks. There I stopped. I pointed down to the earth, into that ditch. I said to Marianne, "Here is where I played out. Here is where I cocked my revolver and fired up into the sky as I was falling back on my head. Here is where I thought I was going to die."

She moved close to me, taking my arm in her two hands. I could feel her shiver slightly. In that peaceful, moonlit night it was a hard dream to remember. But it had happened, nevertheless.

I pointed off at an angle from the tracks, toward a squalor of little adobe houses. "Somewhere in there," I said, "were where two little old ladies lived. Two little old ladies who came and got me out of this ditch. I reckoned they'd heard my revolver firing into the night. But they came and got me and hid me and nursed me back to health. I wish that I could have found them to give them just repayment for giving my life back to me. But I reckon that's a debt so big that a man can't ever really repay it."

She clung to me closer. I stood there, looking a moment more at the place my life was supposed to have ended, and then I took her gently by the waist and said, "All right, let's go back to the carriage. This is finished."

We got back in and I told the driver to take us to the middle of the International Bridge. My mood was down and I desperately wanted to lighten it for her sake. I had promised to show her Mexico; instead, I'd shown her a piece of my past. And not a very good piece to look at, either.

As we were rolling through town, I said, "Listen, do you want to stop and go to a cantina? Maybe see some of the night life in such a place?"

But she shook her head. She was still clinging to my arm. She said, "No, I want to talk to you tonight. I think that's what I want to do."

I patted her hand that was holding the upper part

of my arm. I said, "Well, I promised you a good time, but I really didn't see to it. Maybe I will next time."

She said, "I think I understand."

When we got to the middle of the bridge, I told the driver to stop and we got down. I said, "We can walk back from here."

There was a wooden railing along the side of the bridge, and we walked over to that and I leaned up against it. The moon was up good and making a streak on the slow-moving water of the river. We were still less than halfway across, still on the Mexican side. I said, "Do you know what this river is called?"

She said, "Of course. It's the Rio Grande."

I shook my head. "No, that's wrong."

"You're crazy. I know it's called the Rio Grande. Everybody knows that."

I said, "You're standing in the wrong place for it to be the Rio Grande. Where you're standing it's the Rio Bravo."

"Will, what the hell are you talking about? Now, is or is not this goddam smelly river named the Rio Grande?"

I said, "Well, if we were to walk forward about a hundred yards it would be." I was laughing a little, glad to have the chance to get a little of the blackness out of my mood.

But I'd teased her long enough. I said, "This river is called the Rio Bravo in Mexico and the Rio Grande on the Texas side. I don't know why that is, but that's a fact."

She said, "Oh, you're just funning me. A river can't have two names."

"You bet it can," I said. "Just like a man can have

two names. You call me sweetheart, but I reckon if we were to look up a lawman over there in Laredo and ask him what he called Wilson Young, it damn sure wouldn't be sweetheart."

She said, "Will, what led you into this life?"

I shook my head. "I don't know. And by the time I was old enough to have sense enough to want out it was too late. Cm'on, let's start walking back across."

We reached the end of the bridge and stepped onto Texas soil. Our hotel was only a few blocks away, but I wasn't ready to go there right then. I wanted to tell her what had happened between me and Austin Davis. I wasn't ashamed of what I'd done, but I did want her to know what had caused my bad mood and what I'd done about it. I figured I was maybe fixing to get in trouble, for I didn't think she was a woman who was going to take too kindly to being mistrusted, especially after all she'd given up to be with me and all the risks she'd already taken for my sake.

But they say confession is good for the soul.

So, instead of walking her back to the hotel, I aimed us toward the plaza. We arrived and sat down on one of those concrete benches, and I got out a cigarillo and lit it. After a minute I said, "Marianne, sometimes I ain't as tough as I seem to be."

She said, "Well, is anybody?"

"What I mean is, maybe I worry about some things you wouldn't expect me to worry about."

"What are you talking about, Will?"

Well, I was starting to lose my nerve. So I just shook my head and said, "Nothing, I reckon. Just kind of rambling." I drew on my cigarillo. "I guess coming back here to Nuevo Laredo made me think about the passage of time. Guess I'm just getting older. Or old, or something. Hell, I don't know." I got up. "Let's go back to the hotel and have a drink."

We walked on back. She was, I think, considerably troubled by what my mood had been most of the day and the evening. Well, I didn't think I was going to tell her much more. We went on in the hotel lobby and then through the door into the little bar. It was starting to get late and there were only a few patrons standing up to the bar and none at the tables. One of the men at the bar was Austin Davis. Marianne and I took a table. About the time we got seated Austin looked around, but all he did was give us a little nod. Then he finished his drink, paid his score, and walked out.

Marianne said, "That was your friend. How come he didn't come over?"

I said, "Because I threatened his life this afternoon if he ever looked at you again."

She said, "You did what!" She was staring at me, her eyes round.

So I went ahead and told her, just told her the whole goddam story from beginning to end. I had to stop at one point for the waiter to bring us a bottle of brandy and a couple of glasses. I poured us one out and took a drink of mine, but Marianne never touched hers, just sat there staring at me waiting for me to finish.

I said, "So that's what had me in the mood I was in up in the room."

She said, "Well, I'll be go to hell. Goddam, you never cease to surprise me."

I looked at her. She was staring at me with set eyes. I said, "Now don't start on me, Marianne. I already feel a little like a fool. I don't need no help from you."

She shook her head quickly from side to side. Then she said, "I guess I should have figured it from the way you acted in Houston. You're as tender as a baby."

I said, "What's that supposed to mean?"

She put her hand on mine. "That's all right, honey," she said. "I'll not ever make that mistake again. I'll see to it that you never have cause to be jealous over anything again. I understand better now."

I was so astonished I didn't know what to say. I'd thought she was going to be mad as hell; instead, I'd gotten something quite different on my plate. It kind of embarrassed me. I had finished my first glass of brandy so I poured me out another. She still hadn't touched her first. Then I raised my glass and said "Luck" and she done likewise and we both knocked them straight back as befits the toast.

After that I paid the score and we went on upstairs. Walking up I was still kind of thoughtful. Me and Marianne had come a long way in the few months since I'd met her. Question was, where were we going?

We got in the room and I propped a chair under the knob like I always did and then went over and poured myself out a drink of brandy. Marianne undressed and put on her robe and then lay down on the bed. I took off my boots and my gun belt and then sat down on the chair in front of the window and looked out on the streets of Laredo.

She had a pillow propped under her head and was laying there watching me. I was thinking about Wilcey and Chulo. I was going to meet them next morning at a cafe we'd selected as we'd come into town. To tell you the truth, I didn't even really know where they were staying. I didn't think it was going to be necessary for us to all act like we didn't know one and another, but I did figure to kind of hold down on the times we were seen together. It was a fact that I was the most wanted and the most well-known, and there was no use them getting caught in the same net if the law was to get onto me. I was thinking about just that when Marianne asked me how dangerous I thought it was for me to be in Laredo.

I shrugged and said, "I'll tell you the same thing I told Wilcey. It's dangerous wherever we are. Laredo ain't no worse than San Antonio or Houston or even the Panhandle, for that matter. Or California. For we're wanted out there from a trip in that direction some three or four years back."

She said, talking with the side of her head on the pillow, "Will, what will you do if they ever catch you?"

I said, a little sharply, "Now I don't want any of that kind of talk. It don't lead to no end. Maybe they will catch me someday, but I ain't going to worry about it right now. I've been chased, but never caught. I've been shot, but never killed. I have wanted notices hanging on walls in every jail across this state. But I never been in any of those jails. So I'm just going to trust to my luck and go ahead."

I sipped my drink and she lay there looking at me. After a moment I said, "What I'm worrying more about than anything else is what I'm going to do about you."

"What do you mean?"

I looked out the window for a minute, seeing the night and the deserted streets. Then I looked back at her. "What I said. What am I going to do about you." I sipped at my drink. I said, "I'm a man on the run,

Marianne. What the hell do I have to offer you? What kind of peace can I give you? Hotel rooms and cafes and the ever-constant fear something will happen to me? That I'll be shot, killed? What kind of life is that to offer a woman." I looked down at the floor. "I don't know a safe place to put you. I can't stand the idea of giving you up, but I don't know what to do with you. I've been dreading talking about this ever since San Antonio."

She sat up on the side of the bed. "Wait a minute," she said. "I got something to say about what you do with me. It ain't just your decision, cowboy."

"So? What bright idea have you got?"

She said, "Nothing has to be done with me. This isn't bothering me. I'm a big girl. I knew what I was doing when I came away with you. I knew what I was doing when I left Galveston for you. Don't you think about putting me someplace, some safe place, as you say. Because I won't go. I want to be with you."

I said, with a little effort, "That might not always be possible. Marianne, you got to think about this seriously. This ain't right. Something could happen to me at any time. I—"

She suddenly slid down off the bed and was on her knees in front of me. She said, "No! You're the best! No one can hurt you."

I shook my head. "Maybe in a fair fight. Maybe for now. But, remember, I'm almost thirty-five years old. I'm going to start to slow down. I won't always be the best. And that really doesn't make any difference. Any drunk, who goes crazy and decides to make a name for himself by killing Wilson Young can shoot me in the back of the head."

"But you don't ever let anyone behind you."

Well, I smiled a little at that, for you can never be sure someone isn't behind you. I said, "All right, then, shoot me in the chest from across the bar. I can't watch everything. And everybody."

She hit me on the knee with her little fist. "I don't want to hear this. Don't talk like this. No one can kill you! You're Wilson Young."

I said, "Yeah, but everybody don't know it." I sipped at my brandy again and then very reluctantly told her about the boys that tried to rob us on the road. I said, "So you see, I was a fraction of an inch from being killed by a nervous young kid. He didn't know I was Wilson Young. But he could have killed me all the same."

"Oh, hell!" she said. She put her face in her hands. "Let's don't talk anymore. I don't want to hear anymore. This has been a hell of a day. Let's go to bed and go to sleep!"

"No," I said, a little sharpness in my voice. "I want you to understand what I feel I'm up against." I pointed at her suitcase. When I'd come in I'd brought my saddlebags with the money in it and shoved it into her suitcase. I said, "That's a good example right there. That money I put in your suitcase, that's the only kind of security I can offer you. What's that to hold out to a woman. For hell's sake, Marianne, I can't even put my money in a bank! What kind of a way is that to live?"

She suddenly grabbed my free hand in both of hers. She looked up at me, fiercely. She said, "Will you stop this goddam talk! I don't care! I can't think of living without you, dammit! Now let's go to bed! I'm so damn tired I don't even know who I am. Goddammit, Wilson, you have put me through a wringer this day, you and your moods! I thought we were down here to have some fun. Now let's go to bed and rest some. Talk about this another day."

I looked down into her face. After a second I said, "All right." I drained my glass of brandy. "Put out the light while I get undressed. We'll sleep."

Chapter Four

Chulo and Wilcey were already in the cafe when I showed up the next morning. They'd already been brought their coffee and had a bottle of bourbon whiskey sitting there on the table. I sat down and ordered coffee and then gave them a good morning.

I said, "Well, I hope ya'll been managing to stay out of trouble."

Wilcey said, kind of sourly, "We been doing all right."

Chulo said, "I fuck plenty weemen."

I looked at him and kind of shook my head. "Chulo, I think we are going to get you cut. Either that or put you out to stud at a price."

Wilcey said, "You been doing all right?"

I nodded.

"How's Marianne?"

"She's fine."

Just then the waiter brought my coffee and I took

time to pour a little bourbon in it and to take a few sips. Then I said: "Where ya'll staying?"

Wilcey named a little hotel I remembered the name of. It was just a few blocks down the street.

Then he said, still kind of sourly, "What I want to know is, what are me and Chulo supposed to be doing while you and your lady are having a good time? Just waiting?"

I said, "Well, I thought we'd all go over tonight to Nuevo Laredo and have a meal together. Would that suit you?"

He said, "Ya'll going to hold hands at table?"

I didn't say anything to that. I knew what made him say it. Instead, I said, "And I got an idea for a little piece of business I think we need to discuss. I think it's what we're going to do after we leave here."

"What?"

"I ain't going to talk about it now. Let's talk about it tonight. But, and I swear it, it's the best goddam idea I ever had for doing some business."

He said, "Here?"

"No, dammit, not here. I done told you that."

"Where, then?"

"I'll tell you when the time comes. Let's finish our breakfast."

The waiter had brought our breakfasts, and for a little, I devoted my time to the food. Then Wilcey said, "I seen your old partner just a little while ago."

I looked up at him. I said, "Who are you talking about?"

"That Austin fellow." He looked over at Chulo. "What was the hell of his name, Austin something?"

Chulo didn't say anything and he said, "Austin Dallas? What was it?"

I gave him a sour look. "Davis. Austin Davis. You damn fool. Where'd you see him?"

I said it with such heat that it kind of surprised him. He said, "Well, hell, here. Right here in this cafe. Right before you come in. He was here when we got here. About to leave."

I said, "Yeah? What'd he have to say?"

"He didn't have nothing to say. Just kind of give us a nod and went on about his breakfast and then left. Why?"

"Nothing," I said. "Just nothing."

Well, nobody had much to say after that. We kind of ate the rest of our breakfast in silence. I guess, mainly, because I was kind of deep in thought and Wilcey could always pick up on my mood and Chulo never had much to say anyway.

When it was over, I said, "Well, I'll see ya'll at your hotel in about three or four hours. Then we'll make plans to go across the border and have a little good times."

Wilcey said, "What are you fixing to do?"

"Nothing," I said. "Goddammit, all I'm going to do is go back to the hotel and maybe walk Marianne around a little and go to lunch. Is that all right?"

He kind of growled, "Well, whatever. Just you be kind of careful."

I said, "What is all this careful stuff? I been careful all my life. Will you quit being an old woman?"

He said, "I ain't never been in Laredo with you before."

I said, "Cut it out."

THE TEXAS BANK ROBBING COMPANY

After we paid our score I walked on back to the hotel. It was a fine, early summer day and I was in mighty good spirits. Me and Marianne had resolved our differences and I didn't see a thing that was wrong with the world. I walked on into the hotel lobby and then thought I'd have one other drink before I went on upstairs, so I stepped into the little bar that was just a few steps off to the right. The minute I walked through the door I saw Austin Davis sitting at a table over near the back wall, drinking all by himself. He looked up when I walked over. I said, "Mind some company?"

He kind of shrugged and shoved a chair out with his boot. "Make yourself at home. It's a public place."

I sat down. He had a bottle of bourbon on the table, but only one glass. I sat while he signaled the bartender to bring another glass for me. When it came he uncorked the bottle and poured me out a drink. He was already into his so we didn't make a toast. I just picked mine up, drank off about half, set it back down, lit up a cigarillo, and then leaned back in my chair. He was just kind of sitting there, not looking at me or much of anything. I said, "Well, how's Laredo treating you?"

He said, "About as well as I'm treating it."

Well, there wasn't much I could say to that. I felt a little awkward. Hell, I didn't even know why I'd come over to visit with him; I guess because I'd felt a little wrong about what I'd done. But I ain't much of a man to apologize and I wasn't sure he had one coming, even if I'd knowed how to go about it. So I said, "Hear you run into my partners just a bit ago. Over in that cafe down the street."

He just said, "Yeah."

It was plain he wasn't going to make it easy on me.

I thought in walking over to his table he'd take it as a friendly gesture and respond in kind, but that didn't seem to be what the case was going to be. I said, "Listen, Davis, as much trouble as you and I have had in our life, it don't seem to make much sense that we'd make any for each other."

He looked up at me, then. He said, "Yeah, that's what I was thinking. Right after that little game of ring around the rosy you and me played in the hall of the hotel."

I let it lay. He was kind of baiting me, but I gritted my teeth and just let it alone. I took my drink up and finished it and set my empty glass back on the table. He made no move to refill it. I said, "Well, I got to be getting. I'd just wanted to tell you the one thing."

"Yeah? What?"

I said, "I already told you."

He said, "Oh, yeah? What'd you tell me?"

I felt myself getting a little stiff. I said, "Well, if you didn't hear me the first time, I goddam well ain't going to say it again."

He said, "You told me that me and you had both had too much trouble in our lives to make some for each other. That being the case, how come you came at me with trouble?"

Well, he was starting to make me just a little warm. I'd come over with the best intentions in my mind. I said, "Now just a goddam minute, Davis. I done gone about as far as I'm going to go. I thought you might be fixing to make some trouble for me. I wanted to head it off."

He didn't say anything. Just sat there looking at me. I said, "Listen, I'll say one other thing. And that's all the goddam hell I'm going to say. And if you want to be my enemy as a result of all this, then, by God, that's the way it's going to have to be." I said, "As schoolboy as this may sound, I never felt the way about a woman as I do this one. That's all I'm saying. And I ain't offering it as no goddam excuse! If you think I might have acted a little hastily, then you're just damn well going to have to think that."

I pushed my chair back and started to get up, but he suddenly put out his hand and took up the bottle and poured my glass full. He said, "Hell, Will, what's your rush? Let's have another drink together."

I took a long moment. I looked at the whiskey and I looked at him. His face was dead even straight. I finally said, "All right, what the hell. But pour yourself a full glass. If we're going to drink, let's drink properly."

He nodded and picked up the bottle and helped his own glass. "All right," he said.

I picked up my glass and he done likewise and we said "Luck" and knocked them straight back as befits the toast.

Then I sat there and give him a hard look. I said, "Goddam, Davis, you are a hard man to like."

He give me a kind of startled look. "What the hell are you talking about? I ain't seen you in ten years and then I take some drunk off your back and the next thing I know you got me slammed up against a wall in a hotel. Now you want to tell me who the *hard* man to like is?"

I said, "Oh, yeah, that! But what I'm talking about is something else. Don't you play the calf with me! All your pretty manners! Sweeping off your hat to my woman. Giving her the eye! Don't you come that shit on me. You and your goddam pretty ways."

He looked at me a long moment and then he started laughing. And he kept on laughing.

After a few seconds it started to make me pretty hot. I said, "Now, just what the hell are you laughing at?"

He finally got himself calmed down enough to talk and he said, "Shit, after I come back to this country all I heard about was how tough Wilson Young was. Word was you didn't fuck with him no way, no how." Then he started laughing again.

I said, "Now, goddammit, you better watch yourself."

He said, "And now I find out that he can be scared by a man sweeping his hat off to a woman. His woman. Never mind the pistols, boys, just sweep your hat off to his woman and you got old tough Wilson Young!"

Well, it took me a minute, but I finally seen the humor in the situation myself. I laughed a little. Then I said, "Well, maybe you might be a little right." But then I said, "But, goddammit, if you ever tell that story to anyone!"

And be damned if he didn't start laughing again. I said, "Aw, the hell with you, Davis. Pour us out another drink and then I got to go."

We visited a little while longer and then I went on up to the room. Marianne was up and dressed and sort of getting herself ready for the street.

I said, "What the hell you been doing?"

"Just resting." She came over and gave me a kiss. "I haven't been up all that long. Did you and Wilcey and Chulo have a good breakfast?"

I said, "Yeah," and then I sat down in a chair and told her all about it, including Austin Davis.

She said, "I'm glad about that. But I figured all along you'd get it straightened out in your mind."

I told her we were all going to have supper together, me and her and Wilcey and Chulo. "Maybe not Chulo," I said. "I doubt if he gives the whorehouses over in Mexico a rest long enough to eat."

She give me a look. "And not Austin Davis? Is that right? Is his name Austin?"

I said, "Woman, don't start pranking with me. I am not in a mood for that kind of joke."

She laughed and came over and gave me a little kiss. "I'm going out and do some shopping. There's a few things I want to pick up. Do they have any good shops here?"

I said, "What? What do you mean, good shops?"

She said, "Oh, nice places with good quality merchandise for ladies."

I gave her an astonished look. "Have you lost your mind?"

She said, "No. Why the hell you say that?"

I said, "What in the fuck would make you think I'd know where there are some *nice* shops for *ladies!* Goddam, woman, you may get me broke to halter, but I don't reckon we've seen the day yet where you can ask me a question like that and expect an answer."

Well, we laughed about that a little and then she went on out. I got the bottle of brandy and a glass and turned me a chair around in front of the window and settled down to watch the streets of Laredo and to begin putting my mind on this next job I was thinking about.

Marianne came back after a couple of hours and we spent the balance of the afternoon making a little love and resting and, then, about dusk we went out and sauntered down the street to Wilcey and Chulo's hotel. She waited in the lobby while I went up to their room. Just as I had predicted, Chulo was out tomcatting, but Wilcey was ready to go.

It was a nice evening, pleasant and not too warm so we just decided to walk on across the border. There was a good restaurant that I'd used to eat at, Hallorahans, which was run by an Irish family. That was one thing a lot of folks didn't know and that was that there were a lot of Irish in Mexico. Way I'd heard it one of their past presidents had hired a bunch of Irish mercenary soldiers to keep his own people in line and quite a number had stayed on. As a matter of fact the word *gringo* came from those Irishers. Seemed they had a marching song called, "Green Grow the Lilacs," but of course, those ignorant Meskins hadn't known what they was saying so they'd shortened it on down to Green Grow and from that to *gringo*.

Anyway, it was a good place to eat. We found it across the river and went on in. They had tablecloths on the tables and it was well lit and clean enough to get by.

We got us a table and sat down and ordered up a round of drinks, gave the toast when they came, and then settled down to enjoy a good meal. As I'd figured he would be, Wilcey had been mighty quiet around Marianne. There was nothing I could say to him; women problems is something a man has to work out for himself.

But I did wish he'd loosen up and quit putting a damper on the party.

We didn't have a very good meal. Wilcey wouldn't come out of his mood and there wasn't a hell of a lot to say to him. But finally, we pushed our plates back and he and I lit up cigarillos and he said, "All right. What's this big job you got planned?"

I said, "You ain't going to believe it."

"Why not?"

"Because Chulo gets seasick."

"What's that supposed to mean?"

I said, "You know what happened when we hid him out on that boat in Galveston after he killed the sailor in the bar."

"Whorehouse," he said.

I said, without glancing at Marianne, knowing why he'd said it, "All right, whorehouse. But that ain't got nothing to do with it."

"Well, what are you talking about?"

God knows, I was giving him plenty of slack. Ordinarily I wouldn't have taken his mood for five seconds, but I was giving him some allowance.

I said, "I'm talking about boats. And the water."

"What?"

After we'd robbed the bank in Sabinas Hidalgo, we'd made our escape to Tampico and, from thence, taken passage on a steamer for Galveston. The whole time on that boat I'd taken notice of the rich folks that was our fellow passengers. Judging from some of the rich gowns and jewelry that women were wearing, their men folks must have been carrying a power of money in their pockets. Not to mention what must have been in the safe of the boat itself. At the time it had struck me that there was a killing to be made on that floating bank. But we were on the run then, and the only thing that had been on my mind was to get us to safety.

But since then, it had come to my mind, more than

once, how much good three armed desperados could do in such a situation.

I commenced laying it out for Wilcey.

All he done, of course, just as he always done, was give me a skeptical look.

"You're crazy," he said.

"Why?"

"Hell, you can't rob no ship? Shit!" Then he realized who he was talking in front of and kind of nodded to Marianne. "Excuse me, ma'am."

"Why not?" I asked him.

"Where the hell would you make your getaway? You reckon horses *run* on water?"

I said, "Aw, hell, Wilcey. That's just the way you think. You ain't got no more imagination than an armadillo."

Well, that made him hot. He said, "Well, then, you just tell me how you planning on going about it. Just go ahead. Tell me."

I had it all figured out to a gnat's whisker. First of all that paddle wheel steamer was a shallow draft boat. I knew about that, being from the coast, but Wilcey, being from deep west Texas, wouldn't have known shallow draft from a watering trough. The way I had it figured we'd just overpower what little crew they had, put them in the hold below, subdue the passengers, and just generally take over the boat. After we'd collected all the money and valuables there was to be had, we'd have them land us at some way out-of-the-way point. It being a shallow draft vessel and a coaster, meaning it sailed along right up close to the coast, there was plenty of places we could choose. Then, after they landed us, we'd get lost in the hinterlands and it would be hell's own kind of time before they got to a port and about treble hell's own kind of time before any kind of catch party could come looking for us.

And by that time we would have vanished.

And we'd have picked our landing place in advance and have horses waiting for us there. After that, Satan himself couldn't find us.

I laid it all out for them. There was a silence after I finished. Marianne was the first to speak. She said, "Goddam, Will, that's a hell of an idea. Damn! I don't know nothing about robbing, but if I was going to try, that would be something to my liking."

Wilcey sat there looking at me, rubbing his chin. He finally said, kind of grudgingly, "That don't sound all that bad. But, goddam, Will, that ain't ever been done before, has it?"

I said, "Hell, yes, pirates used to do it all the time. But what the hell has that got to do with it? Everything had to be done that first time. Think about that man that ate the first raw oyster."

I already knew how he felt about raw oysters.

He made a face and said, "Now, cm'on, be serious. This ain't never been done before."

I slammed my fist on the table top. "What the hell's that got to do with it? Nobody had never robbed that big poker game in El Paso. Yet we done it. Nobody had ever robbed that Skillet ranch up in the Panhandle. Yet we done it. Nobody had ever robbed the bank messenger for the Cotton Exchange with them two guards armed with shotguns. Yet we done it. Now you, by God, tell me why this can't be done!"

He said, "But goddam, Will, ain't no cowboys never robbed no ship!"

"I reckon," he said reluctantly. Though I could see it was alien to his nature to even think that way. Wilcey always wanted to know everything in advance. The problem with that was that I couldn't always tell him everything in advance.

He said, "But yeah, when did you figure all of this out? This here seafaring job?"

I said, "You won't believe this, but while I—"

And then I stopped. It would have scared him to know just how fresh all of what I'd thought up had come to my mind.

The truth of the matter was that I'd decided on all of the parts of the job that very afternoon while I'd been staring out the window while Marianne had been shopping. But I didn't want him to know that.

"What?" he said.

"Never mind. It ain't important."

And it wasn't. It didn't matter how I come to the best way to work something; all that mattered was that I had. He wasn't the boss and he didn't have to know all the details until the time came. I was the boss and I took the responsibility for success or failure. That was my cross to bear.

And another thing he'd never know was that I'd decided to work it out so quickly for his sake. I'd seen it was killing him just sitting around, waiting, watching me and Marianne so happy together. I'd known the best thing for him, to get his mind off that goddam Houston woman, was another job. So I'd figured out the boat robbery. It had been in the back of my mind, like I said, for some time. But I hadn't been near about ready to pull it. Not until I seen how bad

Wilcey needed to get back to work. So I'd just sat there and figured it out.

And to tell you the truth, it kind of had me excited.

We all left the table not too long after that and walked on back to Texas. It was a nice evening and we all, including Wilcey, were in a pretty good mood. Halfway across the bridge we stopped and stared down at the water of the Rio Grande. The moon was shining and cutting a long streak down its length. Wilcey said, "Well, there's water. And we're going to rob on water. Damned if I ever thought I could make money on water, other than what I needed to water my cattle back when I was ranching."

Oh, he was in a better mood and no mistake.

When we got back across the border, we split up, Marianne and I to go back to our hotel and Wilcey to go look up Chulo and see what kind of devilry he'd got himself in.

When we got up in the room and I'd got the door jammed good with a chair under the knob, we got undressed and then lay down in bed. I'd poured me a glass of brandy and water and lit a cigarillo, and I lay there with the glass in my hand, sipping at it, and smoking. Marianne was laying very close to me, smelling good and feeling good. To tell you the truth, I was more than just a little bit proud of myself for the plan I'd thought out. I hadn't just gotten Wilcey out of his bad mood, I was pretty sure I'd worked out, with the ship robbery, what to do about Marianne and myself.

She pulled up even closer to me and said: "Will, the robbery plan sounds just wonderful, but what was this you were telling Wilcey about sending me on ahead somewhere to get a place ready to hide out? You never told me anything about that. Where?"

The funny thing about it was that it had been seeing Austin Davis that had brought it to my mind. I'd remembered that, when he'd left Texas with the law and about four husbands on his ass, he'd headed for the Ozark Mountains in Arkansas and hidden out. I said to Marianne, "I'm sending you to Arkansas."

She kind of raised up and looked at me. "Sending me, where? Like hell you are!"

Well, it made me laugh a little. After I settled down, I began to tell her what I had in mind; why it would work and why Arkansas was the perfect place. I said, "You're going up to Yell County. That's where Fayetteville, the capital, is near. But you're going up into the Ozark Mountains and buy us a little place out away from anybody. A place where nobody would ever think to look for us. And I can tell you this about that section of country—you ain't ever going to see a place where people are less interested in their neighbor's business. Folks up there have got too much to hide to be talking about the other fellow. It'll be way off the beaten path, way back in the mountains, the kind of place that nobody is going to go looking for Wilson Young. And ain't nobody up there ever going to have heard of Wilson Young. I'm going to give you enough money, several thousand dollars, so you can just go up there and buy us a little piece of land with a house on it, get it furnished, and be sitting there waiting when I get there."

She said, "Goddam, I could have thought all day and night and never come up with this. Arkansas?"

I said, "Yes."

I took a drink of brandy and a long pull of my cigarillo and began to tell her the best part. All through the years of my outlaw career I'd always looked for that ranch, that other occupation that I could go into to make myself respectable. Well, of course, that had been nothing but a fool's dream. I was going to earn my living as a robber and gunman the rest of my life and there was no two ways about that. So the ideal thing was to face that fact and try to do the best I could with what I had to work with. What I needed was a rest, some time off the owl hoot trail, some time with Marianne. And the only way to do that was to get enough money where we could take two or three years off and hole up in a safe place and get to where we could enjoy life without worrying about a gun being pointed my way at any second. And it seemed like the ship robbery and the hideaway in Arkansas were the answer to the question. We'd have plenty of money and it would give me and Marianne time to enjoy each other and to work out our future without the constant fear that the law was going to come knocking at our door at any second.

Hell, I was tired of sleeping with a cocked gun beside my pillow, tired of listening to every footfall outside the door, tired of waiting for that next fool drunk to recognize me and try and make a name for himself. I wanted me some good times with my woman, and not just a few nights and days, neither, but some substantial time.

I told her as much of this as I could, doing the best with the poor way I have with words, especially when it comes to talking to the woman I love about her and me and being able to spend some time with her in peace and happiness.

When I was through, she just sat right up beside me and looked intently down into my face. She said, a kind of breathlessness in her voice, "Oh, Will, do you mean it? Do you really mean it? I ain't just dreaming?"

I said, "I mean it."

"A place of our own? I mean, I don't care what it's like. A shack. I don't give a damn. But do you really mean it?"

"Yes." I could see her face through the blue haze of the smoke from my cigarillo.

"Goddam!" she said. She kind of sat back and said, "You mean we wouldn't be running? Wouldn't be afraid? We could live like real people?"

Well, that made me laugh just a little. I said, "Yeah, I reckon we could. I reckon we'll have enough money we could get off the owl hoot trail for a good little while. Kind of set up there in Arkansas. Maybe travel up north from there. Visit around. Wouldn't have to do no business, if we were careful, for a good couple of years."

She said, "Goddammit, I don't believe it. Are you serious?"

"Hell yes! Why wouldn't you think I was serious?"

She was kind of settling back. She looked off, staring at the far wall. "Oh, I don't know," she said.

"What the hell you mean, you don't know."

She just kind of shook her head. "Sounds too good to be true."

"What do you mean by that?"

She looked at me. She said, very slowly, "Because I'd taken you for what you were. I'd figured on whatever time I could have you would be a time of running and being afraid all the time. And now this. So soon."

I said, "Hell, why not? How come it can't be sooner than later?"

"Yeah," she said, still slowly. Then she looked at me. "And we'd be really safe up there in Arkansas? In the goddam Ozarks?"

"As in a mother's arms," I said. "Hell, they'd never think to look for me up there and them people don't give a goddam."

"And we'd have a little place of our own?"

"Yep."

"And I could have my own furniture? And my own dishes? And make the house the way I wanted it?"

"Yep," I said. "And I'd get me a brown sack suit and wear a foulard tie and you and me could go to church and you in a little blue gown and a little white hat."

She suddenly grabbed me fiercely. She said, "Goddam you, Wilson Young, I'm going to Arkansas and find that place and I'm going to make you the happiest goddam man that ever lived!"

I just hugged her. Wasn't much else I could say. She pulled away from me and looked in my face and said, "Now you go and rob that goddam ship and get *all* their money! And that place in Arkansas will be waiting. Hell, I'm ready to go right now."

We went to sleep that night feeling mighty good.

Chapter Five

I had made an engagement to meet Wilcey and Chulo the next morning for breakfast to go over the details of the steamer robbery. Wilcey had guaranteed he'd have Chulo there, no matter what kind of shape he was in. So I kissed Marianne good-bye, leaving her comfortable in bed, and set out up the street in a considerable good humor.

They were there, drinking coffee, when I come in, took off my hat, and had a chair. The cafe wasn't too crowded, but there was still a fair crowd of men dawdling over the remains of their breakfasts. We'd taken a table to the back, a table that allowed us to see out the plate glass window of the front of the cafe. Chulo was in the chair that had its back up against the wall. I didn't much like it, but, rather than moving him out, I just went ahead and took one that at least gave me a half view of the room.

I let the waiter come over and bring me coffee,

poured me a little brandy in it, took a sip, and then said: "Well, gentlemen, I fancy we are going to take our chances."

Wilcey said, "I'm ready."

Chulo said, "We rob one Meskin bank?"

For some reason he was always wanting to rob "one Meskin bank." I never could figure out why that was. I said, "No. We rob one boat."

He gave me a kind of blank look. "Boat?"

"Boat," I said. "Ship. Like we left Mexico on."

"Sheep?" He began to look worried. He'd been awful seasick when we'd hidden him out on that little sloop in Galveston after he'd killed the sailor in the bar. He said, "Sheep? Chulo get seek!"

I shook my head. "No, you won't get sick. Or even *seek*. You didn't get sick on the big boat we took, you only got sick on the little one at the dock."

He said, "And this be big sheep?"

"Yes. This be big *sheep*." God, he looked awful. He hadn't shaved and he probably hadn't had a bath in a week and he looked like he hadn't had any sleep for about the same amount of time. He also had some pretty good scratches down one side of his face. I said, "Well, I see you be trying to fuck a wildcat again. When you going to learn that wildcats don't like to fuck. Except other wildcats."

He said, "Aw, Weel. Chulo ain't been fucking no wildcats. Chust girls."

"Hmmmmp," I said. I turned to Wilcey. "Well, you about ready to head south?"

He said, "I could leave today for that matter. But I reckon you and your bride want to stick around here a couple more days and love it up. Can't say I blame you."

But there was still a little bitterness in his voice, the bitterness of a man without a woman. I knew just how he felt. God knows, I'd felt that way often enough in my own past.

Then I noticed Wilcey was looking intently over my shoulder, toward the window of the cafe.

I turned and looked, but didn't see anything except a few casual passersby out on the boardwalk. I said, "What?"

He shook his head. "I don't know. For a minute I thought I saw those boys."

"What boys?"

"Aw, them would-be road agents. Them boys that tried to rob us."

"Hell you say." I turned and looked again, but didn't see anything. I said, "You sure?"

"Naw, not really. I saw some faces peering in the window, and I thought it was them for a second. But the sun was hitting the glass all wrong and I couldn't really tell."

I shrugged. "Hell, them boys are probably clean to Corpus Christi by now." I signaled for the waiter to come over. I said, "Let's have a little more coffee."

But Wilcey was getting up. "I've had my fill. We're going to saunter up the street. You coming?"

"Naw," I said. They'd started before I'd got there and I hadn't had enough coffee and brandy to get me going of a morning. I said, "I'll sit here a while longer. I'll catch up with ya'll before the day's out."

They left and the waiter came over with some fresh coffee and I helped it out from the bottle of brandy

THE TEXAS BANK ROBBING COMPANY

and then lit a cigarillo and sat there smoking and sipping and feeling just pretty damn good. I was kind of starting to wish old Austin Davis would come along. I felt like we'd patched up our differences, but it wouldn't have done us no harm to have drank a little more whiskey over them.

I thought about moving around to the seat against the wall that Chulo had vacated, but I was feeling so content I didn't feel like stirring myself. I sat there, not thinking about much of anything, just feeling pleasant about the way it looked like things were going to work out. To tell you the truth, I wasn't even much worried about robbing the ship and then making a successful getaway. Which ain't the regular way for me. Normally, I'm plenty worried about every job and I agonize over every last little detail, always convinced I've forgotten some little something that's going to get us all killed. But in this case I thought that surprise was going to be so on our side, and the people we'd be robbing so unprepared for such a job, that it was just going to be a piece of cake. I knew for a fact that something like it had never been done, at least by cowboys as Wilcey called us. Pirates, of course, but from another ship. Hell, the crew of that boat would never know what hit them. We'd have them in the cellar of that ship and locked up so fast they'd never even be able to get their breaths. And after that, we'd just take our pickings. And they ought to be pretty thick pickings, too. Enough where me and Marianne would just be set up for quite a little while.

And thinking about that, thinking about getting off the owl hoot trail and not having to be on the run and the hide and the shoot all the time just gave me an uncommon feeling of relief.

It was with these good thoughts in my mind that I suddenly felt something hard pressed up against the back of my head and a voice saying, "Don't move! You're dead if you move!"

I stiffened, caught completely unawares, unsure about what was happening or what to do. In that instant two men, both holding shotguns, suddenly jumped into my vision, one on each side of me.

They had badges on their chests. They were law. They pointed the shotguns straight at my breast.

The moment that I had dreaded and had feared for so many years had finally come about. I was under arrest.

In that instant such a flood of anguish and despair came over me that, even with the two shotguns from the front and the one from the back pointed at me, my hand nearly flew down for my revolver. But I hesitated an instant too long, for two other men suddenly grabbed me by the arms and jerked me to my feet.

I could dimly hear yelling, dimly feel the power of the hands holding me, but, so deep was my sudden helplessness and panic that it was as if everything was taking place in a fog bank.

Behind me I heard a man yelling, "Get them irons on his wrists! And get that goddam gun out of his holster!"

I struggled, shoving and throwing my shoulders back and forth, trying to free my hands. But it was no use. I couldn't out-strong a man on each arm. And even while I tried more hands came to help those that already held me. I thought, God, how many are there to take just one man!

I yelled out, "Goddammit! What is this? Are you crazy! Turn loose of me, goddammit!"

But of course, they wouldn't. I felt the handcuffs go around my wrists, felt them snapped in place. The voice behind me said, "All right, turn him around. But watch him, goddammit!"

My mind had gone numb, something that had never happened to me in a moment of crisis or danger before. All I could feel was the confinement of the irons on my wrists and the hands on my arms and shoulders. I tried to struggle as they whirled me around to face the man who'd been talking behind me.

He was tall, with a belly protruding over his belt. He had a shotgun in his hand. It was pointed right at my chest. I figured it was he who'd first stuck a gun up against the back of my head. He had a badge on his chest. He was gray haired, with a lined face and a big nose. The hands that held the shotgun were shaking slightly.

I said, "What the goddam hell is this! Turn me loose!"

He said, and there was a slight quiver in his voice, "You're Wilson Young, the outlaw, and, as sheriff of Laredo, Texas, in the county of Webb, I arrest you!"

"Shit!" I said. "I ain't Wilson Young, whoever that is. My name is Jim Wilson and I can prove it. Now you goddam well better turn me loose or I'm going to law and sue you for false arrest!"

He said, "You're Wilson Young! There's a poster of you in my office and the description fits you to a T!"

I said, "Say, who the hell are you? I want your name for the goddam lawsuit I'm fixing to file against you!"

"My name is Tom Langley and I'm the sheriff of Webb County. And you're Wilson Young. And you're wanted in about a dozen counties, including this one."

I said, "You're full of shit, that's what you are. Now you get these goddam irons off my wrists and tell your goddam deputies to take their hands off me and I might be willing to forget all this."

The sheriff turned his head and looked back. "Bring them boys up here! Then we'll see what he says."

There was such a crowd jammed around us that whoever he'd sent for was having a hard time getting through. Looking over the heads of the men that were thronging around I could see Chulo standing in the doorway. It give me a start and I commenced praying that Wilcey was with him and that he wouldn't do anything foolish. I still had hopes I might talk my way into a place where I could break my bonds and make my getaway. Or else there was still the chance that I might bluff the sheriff into believing he'd made a mistake.

But then the crowd parted and them same three goddam boys who'd tried to rob us were being pushed forward. They were being pushed because they were trying to cower back. I stared hard at them, but none of them would meet my eye. I said, "What's this shit? Three snot-nosed kids?"

But the sheriff wasn't paying any attention to me. He said, to the boys, "Now don't be afraid. He can't hurt you, just like I said. Now, is this Wilson Young?"

The crowd had fallen back so that they stood there side by side, just to the left of the sheriff. They still wouldn't look at me directly, just kept taking little quick glances at me like it might kill them if I got a chance to bore into them with my eyes.

The sheriff said, "Well, is it? Is this Wilson Young?"

They all made quick little nods. But the sheriff said, "Say it aloud. Is it?"

They all kind of mumbled "Yessir" and seemed to want to back up as soon as they'd said it.

I said, "Aw, hell, cut out this shit! You got the wrong outlaw. Them three kids tried to hold me up on the road outside of town when I was riding in day before yesterday."

The sheriff said, "That ain't the way they told it. Seems you robbed them of their firearms and their horses and what little money they had on them. It was you done the robbing."

I kind of laughed, even though it made me plenty hot to be accused of robbing three kids. I said, "Well, I don't know who this Wilson Young is, but if he robs children, he ain't much of an outlaw."

"Well," the sheriff said, "from what I know of you you've done just a few more things. All the way from robbing banks to singing too loud in Sunday school."

I said, "Goddammit, I'm telling you I ain't this fellow you think I am. What the hell makes you want to take the word of these three boys? How the hell they supposed to know?"

The sheriff said, "Because you told them! When you was holding them up you told them your name was Wilson Young!"

Well, that was disheartening. Wilcey had been right. I shouldn't have shot my mouth off and told the boys what my name was. But I'd been so damn angry I just hadn't thought.

Still, it's just such carelessness that will finish you in the outlaw business. You either watch your every word and every move or you'll end up either hung or in the fix I found myself in.

I said, "You ain't going to take the word of three snot-nosed kids, are you? Why, ain't a court in Texas would take that for support of your evidence."

The sheriff said, "Oh, I reckon we'll do better than that. I'll get a wire out to every law man in this part of the country that I've got you in jail and I don't reckon we'll be short of witnesses who'll come forward. And meanwhile, the word of these boys is enough to hold you. Now, we've talked enough. You're coming with us. Bring him on, boys."

There was no point in resisting. When I was pushed forward, I went, holding my manacled hands in front of me. The three boys went scuttling backward as soon as I moved. I gave them a hard eye, but they never seen it, so immediate was their haste to get out of my path.

The crowd fell away, making a clear path to the door, and we went toward it, deputy sheriffs with shotguns on every side of me. I said, to the sheriff, "You sure you got enough men here? Why don't you send for the cavalry? I'm a rancher from Matagorda County and I'm probably the most dangerous man in the world."

He said, "You just come along quietly."

So we walked to the cafe door and out it. Wilcey and Chulo were standing on the sideway, in among the onlookers and curious. They neither made any sign, except Chulo seemed to nod his head toward the cafe, as if to say, "I have seen those boys and they will be taken care of."

Which I didn't much want to happen. But there was nothing I could say at that moment.

We passed on by, turning up the sidewalk. There was as big a crowd gathered around as if they'd come to see a circus. I felt like a damn fool walking through all those staring eyes wearing the irons of a criminal.

But there was nothing I could do about that. The deputies on each side of me had me by the arms. I shook loose. I said, "Take your goddam hands off me! What are you doing, playing heroes for the crowd? You expect me to outrun those shotguns? Goddam!"

The sheriff, who was walking in front, looked back and said, in a loud voice, "You take it easy there, prisoner! It'll go a lot easier on you if you don't give us no trouble."

I was disgusted. I said, "You running for office, sheriff? Trying to scout a few votes up by arresting an innocent man?"

Then, to my left, as we were passing through the crowd, I saw Austin Davis. He was standing at the edge of the street, watching silently. He made no sign, nor did I.

After a block the crowd thinned and the sheriff led us to the middle of the street. I figured he done that so we'd make a better sight and get him more votes the next election.

It was three blocks to the jail from that damned cafe and every foot of it felt as if I were going to my own hanging. I had been numb from the shock of my arrest, but now my brain was beginning to wake up, and I began to feel an almost indescribable panic.

But of course, there was nothing I could do. Even if I hadn't of been handcuffed, there would have been no chance to break away from my confinement. There were too many deputies with too many shotguns. So all I could do was march along as a prisoner and wonder what was about to happen to my life.

We got to the jail and the sheriff threw open the door with a flourish and said, "Inside, prisoner!"

I said, "Oh, go to hell."

But I went on in, walking through the door awkwardly with my hands in irons in front of me. The deputies came crowding in right behind me and the sheriff went and got behind his desk. He said, "You boys watch that door and them winders. Likely he's got friends here and right now is just about when they'd like to ketch us off our guard."

Then he motioned at me. "Prisoner, stand up here in front of this desk."

One of the deputies pushed me forward so that I was facing the sheriff. He said, "Now, take his irons off, but keep them scatter-guns pointed at him and keep 'em cocked. I've heard all about how fast this one is."

I said, while they were taking the irons off me, "Sheriff, am I the first man you ever arrested? You know, for a grown man, you're acting mighty damn foolish."

"Just never you mind all that," he said. "I know what I'm about here. That's why I'm the sheriff and you're the prisoner."

I was looking carefully around me, not that there was that much to see. I hadn't seen too many sheriff's offices and jails, but I figured this was about a run-of-the-mill one. It was a big room with a door opening out to the street and a door in the middle of the back wall that led, I figured, to the cells. There were two desks: the sheriff's and another one I guessed was used by his deputies. There were wanted posters tacked up to the wall, but I didn't see any that looked like me. Besides the sheriff I counted five other law men. I didn't know if they were all his regular deputies or just citizens he might have sworn in for the occasion. Five seemed like too many for a town the size of Laredo, but still, it was a pretty rough little town, and you never could tell how much law the local populace figured to need to protect themselves from all the bad men.

The sheriff was looking through some papers in his desk drawer. Finally, he found what he was after and came out with it and put it on top of his desk. At the top, in big letters, I could see my name: WILSON YOUNG.

The sheriff said, "I knew I had that here somewheres. Now, by God, let's just see how close this is." He studied it, forming the words with his lips and glancing up at me every once in a while. Finally, he nodded and kind of chortled. "Yessir! That's you to a T. Wilson Young, by God, and Tom Langley is the man that caught him." He looked up at me. "How long the law been chasing you, Young?"

I shook my head. "You're talking to the wrong man. I tell you, I'm Jim Wilson, a rancher from Matagorda County."

"Here, that old dog won't hunt, Young!" He tapped the poster. "This is you to your shadow. Same height, same weight, same build, same color of hair and eyes." He gestured. "And look at the way you've got that holster rig set up. That ain't the way a rancher wears a shooting iron. Listen, I know a pistolero when I see one, and you're one if ever there was one." He snorted. "You're about as much rancher as I am Baptist preacher. Now, why don't you be a good fellow and go ahead and own up to who you are. You know we're going to prove it by and by. Why not save us all a lot of trouble and admit it."

I said, "I'll admit my name's Jim Wilson. And that's all I'm going to admit."

For just an instant I thought I saw a little flicker of doubt run across his face. But then he shook his head and said, "All right, be hardheaded. I'll just go ahead and do this thing by the law." Then he kind of straightened in his chair and said, "Prisoner, I charge you with being the well-known outlaw Wilson Young, the per- perperpetrator of a lot of robberies and killings and other depredations and you will be incar- incar-, jailed here until you can be taken before a judge and jury and tried for your misdeeds. Now, Young, empty your pockets out here on this desk."

I said, "My name is Jim Wilson. But all I've got in my pockets is a little cash."

He said, "Have it your own way. Just empty your pockets."

I got cash out of my pants pockets and cigarillos and matches out of my shirt pocket. It was all I had on me. I'd even left my pocket knife laying back on the bedside table at the hotel.

The sheriff reached out and got my roll of money and counted it. He whistled. "Little over four hundred dollars here. Lot of money for a rancher to be carrying."

One of the deputies said, "Well, he won't be needing it. Not where he's going. That'll buy us a lot of whiskey."

I said, "Now just a goddam minute, sheriff. What do you intend doing with that money? While I'm in your goddam jail there's liable to be some things I want to buy. You ain't got no right taking my cash away from me."

He put up his hand. "Now just hold on. Nobody's stealing your money. It'll be right out here kept safe for you. If they's anything you want to buy and I'm willing to let you have it, why all you got to do is ask for some of your money." He glanced away from me toward the window. "Archer, get your goddam head swiveled back around! You're supposed to be watching out that window. Not paying attention to this business in here." He came back to me. "Now get over there and sit down in that chair and take your boots off."

I looked at him. "You going to make me go barefoot?"

"No, but you wouldn't be the first I ever seen was carrying a boot gun. Just get on over there and do it."

While I was taking my boots off he said to his deputies, "Boys, just to make sure you stay on your toes about this one. That poster said there was a fifteen-hundred-dollar reward on his head for his arrest and capture, dead or alive. And that's just one poster. I bet they's others."

One of the deputies whistled. "That's a power of money."

When I'd finished taking off my boots, one of the deputies inspected them like he thought a rattlesnake was fixing to jump out. Then another patted me down to make sure I wasn't carrying a concealed cannon, I guess. When it was over with they let me put my boots back on. I gestured at my cigarillos and matches lying on the desk. "You going to keep my smokes?"

The sheriff picked them up and held them out to me. "No, you can get these. Hell, Young, we ain't savages or Meskins."

"Thanks." I stuck them back in my shirt pocket.

The sheriff got up and took a ring of keys out of a desk drawer. He looked at me. "Time to lock you up."

I just looked at him. Those were words I'd vowed I'd never hear. I'd vowed no one was ever going to put me in jail, that I'd die first. Yet they'd taken me so unawares that I'd never really had no selection, not unless I'd just wanted to be shot down in cold blood.

Well, when he said that, I resolved, right then and there, that they weren't going to hold me. I didn't know how I was going to get out, but I was.

The sheriff looked at one of his deputies. "Claude, you and I will take him on back. The rest of you watch the front of this place and I don't mean maybe."

He unlocked the door that led to the back and we went through, the sheriff leading and the deputy he'd called Claude bringing up the rear carrying a shotgun. Claude looked to be about a double for the sheriff, although he appeared to be about ten years younger and maybe ten pounds fatter.

Through the door I could see there were about eight cells, four on each side. There were solid walls between each cell, but the fronts were open except for the bars. We walked down the corridor between the cells. There was one old man in a front cell. He raised up from his bunk as we passed, looking curiously at us. Then, about halfway down, there were what appeared to be a couple of Mexican cowboys. They looked like they was just waking up from a hell of a hangover and was wishing they'd never come to town.

Other than that the place was deserted. The sheriff said, "I'm going to turn them Meskins loose today. After that it'll be just you and the old man. I can't turn him loose, much as I'd like to."

They led me to the last cell on the right. The sheriff opened the door and then stepped aside and motioned for me to go in. He said, to his deputy, "Claude, you stay back here and keep us covered with that scattergun. I'm going to have a private word with Mr. Young here."

I went over and sat down on the little bunk bed they had in there and lit up a cigarillo. The sheriff stood just inside the door, kind of leaning against one jamb. He said, "Now, Wilson, ain't no reason you and I can't get along. I know you ain't feeling too good about being in here and I don't blame you none for that. But if you'll try to get along with me and not cause no trouble, why I'll see to it that you're just as comfortable as we can make you. Within the law, you understand."

I looked at him. I said, "Just how the hell am I supposed to cause you any trouble?"

"Well," he said, "don't get to cutting up or yelling or giving my deputies a hard time. This is just a job for them. You got to understand that. Ain't a one of us bears you any personal feelings. From what I've heerd about you, you always been a pretty good fellow."

I said, "Well, just how you planning on making me comfortable? In a goddam jail cell?"

He nodded. "I don't blame you for feeling that way.

But, like I say, you try and get along with us and we'll do the same for you. You can have smokes and you can have a little whiskey from time to time. And we'll let you send to any cafe you want for your grub. Long as you got the money to pay for it, I'll allow you pretty nearly anything within the law. Only one thing—"

"And what's that?"

He said, "Well, there'll be, most likely, newspaper fellows coming around wanting to talk to you. If you won't tell them I'm letting you have some special treatment and won't run me down and make me sound like a fool—" He gave me a kind of reproachful look "—like you done in front of my deputies and some of the townspeople. If you'll do that, I'll be as easy as I can."

"How about visitors?"

"Well, of course," he said. "Law says you can do that. But not just all the time, you unnerstan'. And nobody inside your cell 'cept your lawyer. You got a lawyer?"

I said, "Goddam, sheriff, I just been arrested about half an hour. How the hell would I already have a lawyer?"

He nodded his head. "I can see that. You want me to send some around? Some of our local boys? I reckon any of them would be proud to take on your case."

I shook my head. "We'll just let it coast for the time being. I'm still trying to figure out what's done happened to me."

He nodded his head. He had some kind of habit of just kind of ducking it before he come out with what he had to say. Just a short bob down and up. He said, "Reckon you are. Can't say that I blame you. I just want you to know I'm grateful to you. And Tom Langley ain't a man don't pay back a debt."

I looked at him. "Grateful to me for what?"

"Fer being here where I could ketch you. You know you wasn't a'tall wrong when you was jibing me about playing up to the voters. Ketchin' you just about cinches me getting reelected. And I'll tell ya, at my age it's a little late to commence learnin' new tricks. I need another term in office."

I just stared at him for a second. Then I gave a little bark of laughter, with no humor in it. "Glad to do you the good term, sheriff," I said bitterly.

He said, "I reckon I kin unnerstan' how you feel. But you was going to get caught sooner or later anyhow. I'm jest glad it was here."

I looked down at the floor, shaking my head. "Oh, shit," I said.

Sheriff said, "Now you remember what we said. Any of them newspaper fellers come around you won't run me down 'ner paint me the fool. Or with anybody else. In return I'll see you get the best treatment the law allows. I'll tell my boys to show you the respect a man like you deserves."

"Thanks, sheriff," I said dryly. "That's damn nice of you."

He said, "You need anything now?"

I started to shake my head and then said, "Some more cigarillos. 'Cause I don't reckon I'll have anything else to do but smoke. And some brandy. Some good brandy."

He give that little quick nod again. "Ar'right. You might's well be comfortable. I got a feeling you going to be here a good little while. It'll take us a good while to get proper witnesses in from out of town."

I said, "You mean it's going to take you a while to milk this for all it's worth. Is that what you're saying, sheriff?"

He said, "Ain't no call to talk like that. I don't mind you saying it to me so long as it just stays with you and me." He glanced over his shoulder. " 'Course Claude's different. He's my chief deputy and he's got as much at stake as I do."

I said, "Ya'll kin?"

He give that little nod again. "My sister's boy." He reached out and got his hand on the door of the cell. "Well, I got some paperwork to do. I'll see that that whiskey and smokes gets to you. Meanwhile, whyn' you just try and not fret yourself."

"Sure," I said. I looked down at the floor. I didn't want to see him closing that door.

I heard him say, "Let's go, Claude. We got to get busy."

And then I heard the godawful sound of that cell door closing, a sound I'd vowed I'd never hear. Not from the inside. The steel *clunk;* the echoing steel against steel *clunk* it made was the most dismal sound I'd ever heard in my life.

I just sat there looking down at the floor, wondering what, now, was to become of me.

Chapter Six

So I was in jail. I was arrested. What I had feared all my outlaw life had finally come to pass. With the shutting of the outer door such a silence descended over the jail cells like I'd never heard before. For a second I felt panic creeping up on me, a wild desire to throw myself against the bars and hammer my way through them.

But I knew that wasn't going to work. I took a deep breath and tried to get control of myself.

Yet the thought kept pounding itself into my head that I was a prisoner. Me that had chosen to go his own way, to roam free, to have no man as a boss, to go and come as I wanted. Me, that had never been restricted by any bonds, was now a prisoner. Confined to the little space I was in; dependent upon the whim of another man as to whether I could smoke or have whiskey or even stay unmanacled.

I had to fight the feeling that gave me. I had to fight

it hard. For the first ten minutes after the sheriff left I had to have a prayer meeting with my own heart; I had to convince myself that this incarceration wasn't going to be forever, that the day was going to come when I'd once again be free. I had to hold on to that hope, convince myself of it. For, if I couldn't make myself believe it, I'd of had to have done myself in, even if the only way would have been to run headlong into the bars and split my head open so that my brains ran out on the cell floor.

I spent a long several minutes like that after the sheriff left, just staring down at the floor, afraid to lift my head and see my surroundings before I'd gotten ahold of myself. For I knew, if I'd looked too soon at the bounds of my confinement, I'd of gone completely loco.

So I kept my head down and stared at the floor and made myself believe that it was not going to be long before I was a free man again.

In those moments I very carefully would not let myself think of Marianne. That was a situation that I was not near ready to handle, and it was best that I keep her out of my mind.

When I finally raised my head, slowly, I was staring at the blank, dingy wall that separated me from the next cell. There was a bunk up against it, the mate to the one I was sitting on. I swung my head to the left, toward the back wall. It too was blank and dingy except for one barred window, high up enough so that a man couldn't stand and look out it. I looked at that little opening, perhaps three feet by three feet, for a good five minutes. It was my only connection with the outside. In any other direction there was nothing but

THE TEXAS BANK ROBBING COMPANY

jail and confinement; out that window was fresh air and freedom. I just kept staring at it, thinking of the few inches it was. Just those few inches between me and the freedom that I'd taken so lightly, but had so suddenly lost. Just a few inches. But those inches were steel and brick and a man cannot break down steel and brick with his bare hands.

Looking at the window I felt another surge of panic come over me, a surge so strong that I quickly looked back down at the floor, looked down at that floor imagining I was anywhere but where I was, looked down until I had myself under control again so that I could raise my head.

The front of the cell was just bars with a barred door right in the middle of it. You could see right into the cells across the little corridor. And they could see into mine. Even from where I was sitting I could see the two Mexican *vaqueros* lounging on their bunks. Looking at them it went through my heart like a gunshot what the sheriff had said—that he was fixing to turn them loose. There were two sorry Meskin roustabouts, laying out a drunk, and here was I, Wilson Young. And yet it would be they who would be leaving and me who would be staying.

So much for being the big shot Wilson Young. It might get you respect and special treatment off some fat-bellied, office-seeking sheriff, but it goddam sure didn't get you freedom.

I looked at those two Mexicans, laying on their bunks, nursing the *crudos* they had from all the tequila they'd drank the night before and I envied them. I don't know when I'd ever had such a similar feeling before in my life. But in that instant I envied them and would gladly have changed places with them, would gladly have been willing to go back to their ranch work across the border, to their low wages, to their awful food, to their greasy, dirty women, to their servitude under some haughty don, to their misery and poverty.

For, at least, they were free.

I looked at them, thinking of how many rancheros, where I'd ridden up to the door of the big house and gotten down and handed my reins to just one such, who'd come running to take my horse and care for him. And I'd never even noticed the man; never even looked at his face; never even wondered what his life was like.

And yet here I sat envying just one such.

I finally looked around again, seeing the window. I thought of going and looking out it, but instead I lit a cigarillo. I noticed I had only three left and I also noticed I wanted a drink, and wanted a drink badly. I hoped the sheriff was going to be as good as his word and bring me what I'd asked for in a hurry.

But I was tough. I had been born tough, raised tough, and I'd stayed tough.

I had to keep reminding myself of that.

And I could take a jail cell; I could take it without cigarillos and without whiskey. Shit, I could take it without food or water. Goddammit, I was Wilson Young and I was a long ways from being beaten.

I said aloud, startled at the sound of my own voice in all that quiet, "You been in worse scrapes. You'll come out of this one all right."

Finally, I got up off the bunk and took a couple of steps and then stopped and stood there in the middle of the room. Well, one thing, they didn't make them goddam cells big enough where a man was going to get lost trying to find his way back to his bunk. I walked over to the other bunk and sat down on it, wondering if I'd picked the best of the lot to lay my head on. It was just as hard; a thin shuck mattress over rawhide thongs, with a couple of dingy blankets on top if you felt like covering yourself with such.

I got up from there and walked over to the window. The bottom part of it was about six inches above the top of my head. Through the bars I could see the sky and the sun outside, could even hear a little of the clatter of the street. I knew I could reach up and grasp the bars and pull myself up to where I could see outside, but I didn't do that right then. Instead I just stood there, staring at the sky and the sun. Then I heard the outer door open, the one that led into the office, and I thought it might be the sheriff bringing me the brandy. God, I wanted a drink. Just all of a sudden I really wanted a drink. I walked over to the front of the cell.

It was not the sheriff, but his fat nephew, Head Deputy Claude. He came down the corridor, jingling his ring of keys, and stopped in front of the cell of the two Mexicans and opened the door. "All right, *señores*. It's time to *vamoose*. Git up from there, goddammit! Cm'on, ah ain't got all goddam day."

I could see the Mexicans slowly and painfully getting off their bunks and gathering up their few belongings and filing through the door with their heads down.

"Hey, Claude!" I called. "How about that stuff the sheriff was supposed to bring me? I'm near out of smokes and I want a drink."

"It's a-comin', Mr. Young. We ain't forgot you. I'll be right back. Let me get these here hot tamales out the door."

I heard him let them out the door to the office, holler at someone else, and then he was back. He stopped a few yards shy of my cell door, like he was afraid to come too close. He said, "Shur'ff wanted to know did you need anybody got word to where you're at!"

I gave a short laugh. "You mean like my gang? You want them to come walking in to visit?"

Claude gave me a kind of hurt look. "The shur'ff didn't mean nothin' like that. We know you wouldn't do something like that. Naw, he thought maybe you had a loved one somewheres would need to know your whereabouts so as not to worry."

Well, that was even funnier. I said, "You reckon if I had a loved one knew I was in jail then that loved one wouldn't worry?"

"Aw, hell, Mr. Young. You know what we mean."

I said, "Yeah, Claude, I know what you mean. No, tell the sheriff there ain't nobody I want notified. I'm sure word has got around pretty well by now anyway. If it ain't, I'm sure the sheriff is going to see to it."

He said, "Well, it's comin' on to the noon hour. You gettin' hongry? We'll send over to that good cafe where we arrested you if you are. They 'bout the best place in town."

I said, "I'm not hungry yet, and somehow, I don't exactly cotton to that cafe the same as I did. What I mainly want right now is some whiskey. Why don't you go and see about that?"

"I was just going," he said.

He left and I went back over to my bunk and sat down and lit a cigarillo. There were a lot of things I had to start thinking about, but I wasn't quite ready to,

THE TEXAS BANK ROBBING COMPANY

so I just let my mind kind of idle along, trying to keep myself relaxed.

I got up and looked out the window, again resisting the urge to pull myself up so I could see out through the bars. I had to save treats like that; I could already tell.

It had kind of surprised me to find out it was just coming the noon hour. I figured I'd been arrested some time around ten of the morning. But that didn't seem like two hours ago; it seemed like about two days ago.

Time was going to pass slowly. That was clear.

I went back and lay down on my bunk and put my hand behind my head and stared up at the ceiling. There I lay, waiting for another man to bring me a drink, unable to get it on my own.

After a while I heard the corridor door being unlocked. I sat up and swung my legs around and started to go to the cell door. But Claude said, "Just hold it right there, Mr. Young. Just stay away from that door."

He'd stopped a little ways from my cell. He had two bottles of brandy under one arm and several boxes of cigarillos in his other hand. There was another deputy right behind him with a shotgun.

I said, "Are you crazy? What do you expect me to do from in here? Throw this goddam cot at you through the bars?"

He said, "Just never you mind. We ain't takin' no chances with you. Shur'ff's orders. You just stand back and I'll slide this here provender in to you."

I stepped back nearly to the wall. He came up to my cell door and slid the whiskey and cigarillos in through the little window where I suppose they slipped your food in, just a little small window in the bars with a metal ledge you could set a plate on. "All right," he said. "There you be."

I said, "I need a glass. And some water."

He gestured toward a back corner of my cell. "Over yonder's a barrel of water. They's a cup in it."

It was just a little wooden barrel. I hadn't noticed it before. Beside it was a bucket, a slop bucket I figured. Well, that was going to be disgusting, taking a shit in a bucket.

I said, "Much obliged."

He said, "Now you sing out when you're ready to eat a bite. And we'll send for it. Shur'ff says for you to holler out you want anything."

My temper suddenly flared a little. I was tired of them jackasses saying I could have anything I wanted. I said, "How about my revolver? How about a rifle? How about a stick of dynamite so I can blow my way out of this goddam sinkhole. Get out of here and quit saying all I got to do is ask for whatever I want! How about a goddam key to that cell door!"

Well, he left in a hurry. I guess I'd hurt his feelings.

I went up to the cell door and got the whiskey and smokes, grateful as a beggar for small change. I opened one bottle, took a quick pull, and then laid the balance of the provender on the cot. Then I went over to the corner and opened the lid of the little water barrel and dipped me up a half cup. The water didn't look none too fresh, but probably, considering the grade of brandy, the whiskey would kill anything that was swimming under a half a pound.

I made me a good stiff drink and then went on back and sat down. I figured I was going to get to know that cot just real well.

THE TEXAS BANK ROBBING COMPANY

For a time I just sat there drinking and smoking. The brandy tasted mighty good, and after I'd got enough in me, it began to feel mighty good.

Without wanting to, I let my mind drift to Marianne. I had tried hard not to think of her, but there didn't seem to be any way to keep her out of my senses. I guess what had been pounding in the back of my mind was what would she do, what would become of her, with me locked away in jail. I knew that I would be a free man someday, but in the meantime, what about her?

Well, it was such anguish, thinking of not seeing her for a long time, maybe never, that I had to quit thinking of it. I couldn't even figure how I'd get word to her. Certainly I didn't expect anyone to come and see me; not Wilcey or Chulo or her. That would be suicide for Chulo or Wilcey and dangerous for her. Not that I even much wanted her to see me in such straits. I think it would have embarrassed me for her to see me locked up and deprived of my freedom.

But what about her? What could I do about her? How could she even get word to me so that I could find her once I broke jail?

Oh, it was all too disheartening to think of so I just rolled off my bed and went and got some more water and added a good shot of brandy to it. Thinking of her had made my mood turn very low. I was dispirited and no mistake.

I tell you, I'd never felt so helpless in my life.

And what of my partners? Neither Chulo nor Wilcey could make it very well without me. Chulo, perhaps, though it would just be a question of time before he got killed or jailed without me there to yank him back from

123

trouble. But Wilcey—he wouldn't have much chance. All he knew now was the outlaw game, but he damn sure didn't know it well enough to get by on his own.

I growled aloud. "Oh, the hell with it!"

Which was a bad sign. I was already beginning to talk to myself and I hadn't been in the lockup a whole day yet.

After a while I yelled for a deputy and ordered up some steak and eggs and coffee from whatever cafe was handy. It came, us going through the same routine of me standing back while they set it on the ledge in the little door window, but I was so down in spirit that I didn't even rag them about how dangerous it was bringing steak in to such a killer as me.

The meal was good, but I could eat very little of it. Finally, I just pushed it away and poured some brandy in my coffee and sat there sipping that. Afterward I lay back on my bunk and covered my face with my arm and tried to doze off.

Of course, sleep wouldn't come. In fact, as jumpy as I was, I doubted I'd ever sleep again.

A funny thing that kept bothering me was the naked feeling I had without my gun belt on. I don't know how many times I put my hand down only to feel my own thigh. I had grown so used to it over the years that the loss of its weight on my right side made me feel as if I weren't walking right.

I guess I finally dozed off, for, the next thing, I heard the sheriff's voice calling to me. I took my hand off my face and opened my eyes. He was standing there at the cell door.

"Sorry to wake you. Was you sleeping?"

I sat up, rubbing my face. "Yeah, I was dreaming I

was out of here and you had a feather up your ass. That way we'd both be tickled."

"Mr. Young," he said, "they's some people here to see you."

I said, "Quit calling me Mr. Young. I done told you my name is Jim Wilson. What people?"

For a second I was alarmed that Wilcey and Chulo and maybe even Marianne had been dumb enough to come into the jail. But I needn't have worried. The sheriff said, "Some of them newspaper fellers. They want to talk to you. Will you do it? Will you let them talk to you?"

I said, "Hell no! Why should I?"

He said, "Aw, Wilson, do it as a favor to me."

I looked at him like he'd been eating loco weed. "Do you a favor? Say, have you forgot you're the hombre stuck me in this goddam jail?"

He leaned forward against the bars, kind of pushing his heavy face against them. He said, "Well, you don't got to. But then I don't got to let you have whiskey in your cell, nor smokes, nor let you send out for your meals."

I looked at him sourly. "Send them in."

"Now you ain't going to bad mouth me?"

"I'm going to tell them you got the wrong man. That I ain't this Wilson Young you keep calling me."

He looked at me for a second. Then he did that little nod of his and kind of grinned. "Well, that's all right. I done told them you'd say that. But I done told them you are Wilson Young."

"Then bring them on."

He started off. Then stopped. "What about you a lawyer? Already a couple of the local fellers come by and said they'd be proud to represent you. Said they'd be real reasonable about their bill."

"Never mind. Never mind. I don't figure to need a lawyer. Bring on your newspaper people."

He started off again and then stopped again. "Oh, now that I think of it. One of them newspaper fellers is local. But they's one from Houston just happened to be in town. He wants to talk to you about some robbery they had done in the past on some such place like the Cotton something or other. He said they had word Wilson Young done it. You mind if he asts you about that?"

I said, "I've never been in Houston in my life."

He left and I sat there wondering how in the hell they could have figured it was me done that robbery on the Cotton Exchange. But then, after I thought about it, it was a pretty easy question to answer. Likely if they'd of had Wes Hardin in the cell instead of me they'd of charged him with the same robbery. Probably every robbery in that part of the country was going to be laid at my doorstep now that they had me caught. It was a hell of a lot easier to accuse a bird in the hand than to go wandering out with a scatter-gun looking for one in the bush to point the finger at.

In a little while I heard them come through the door and then come bustling down the corridor. Naturally the sheriff was leading the way. He pulled up in front of my cell with several gentlemen behind him in straw skimmers and flung out an arm and pointed a finger at me and said, "There he is! There is the desperado, Wilson Young. Wanted all over Texas and half the Southwest and it was Tom Langley brought him to justice."

THE TEXAS BANK ROBBING COMPANY

I just sat there on my bunk, staring at them sourly. If they expected a show they were going to be disappointed.

But they all ganged up there in front of my cell, pressing against the bars and staring in like they were seeing a side show. I just got up, ignoring them, went over to the barrel, dipped me out some water in the cup, and come back over and poured it about half full of brandy. Then I sat there, sipping, staring at them.

One of the gentlemen turned to the sheriff and said, "Is he allowed to have whiskey in his cell?"

I answered before the sheriff could say a word. I said, "It's Texas law, gentlemen. All innocent men are allowed to have whiskey in their cell. I ain't Wilson Young. I am in here by mistake."

Well, that made them take notice. But the sheriff just give a loud hoorah and said, "He's just funning you. This here is Wilson Young, the notorious bank robber, in the flesh."

I said, "That's a damn lie. My name is Jim Wilson and I'm a cattle buyer from Matagorda County. I intend to sue this county and this town for false arrest for all they are worth."

The sheriff give me a reproachful look. "Now, Wilson. Don't mislead these gentlemen."

I said, "Aw, shit. Go to hell."

There were three of them besides the sheriff and besides the deputy he had just down the corridor with the shotgun in his hand. Two of them were pressed up against the bars with pencils and little notebooks in their hands.

One said, "My name is Bailey. I'm with the newspaper here in Laredo. Let me ask you, Mr. Young—did you come to Laredo to rob one of our banks?"

I just stared at him over my cigarillo. I said, "You said your name was Bailey. I never said mine was Young. So quit calling me that and I'll call you by yours. Mine is Wilson. Jim Wilson. And you must be a damn fool. Supposing I was this Wilson Young, whoever he is. Do you reckon I'd be fool enough to answer such a question?" I mimicked his voice. "Did you come to Laredo to rob one of our banks." I looked at him, hard. "Boy, does your mother know you're out on the streets running loose?"

He said, "Then you didn't come to Laredo to rob one of our banks."

I just shook my head and looked down at the floor. "I be goddam," I finally said.

But he went on. "Are you Wilson Young?"

I said, "I done told you. Hell no I ain't Wilson Young. I don't even know who the hell Wilson Young is."

He said, "But you claim you're from Matagorda County, which is in south Texas. How could you live there and not know who Wilson Young is. He's the most famous desperado in this part of the country."

Well, I'd almost made a slip. I said, "Hell, I ain't been here too long. I'm from up in the Panhandle originally. I just come down to that cattle country when the grass begin to play out in west Texas. And we never heard of this here Wilson Young up there."

He commenced writing busily on his little pad. Over his shoulder I could see the sheriff looking anxious. I said, "But I do want to say that if I had to be thrown

THE TEXAS BANK ROBBING COMPANY

in jail I'm glad it was in Tom Langley's. He knows how to treat his prisoners right."

Well, I done it for fun, but it sure put a look of horror over the old sheriff's face. I figured I'd better set it straight real quick or I might have more than a hard time getting a little whiskey sent in. I said, "What I mean is, Sheriff Langley's a hard man, but he's fair. He's fair. A credit to the town. I don't believe I could have been apprehended any faster than he and his men done it."

Well, they weren't paying the slightest bit of attention to that, but it did make the sheriff beam just a little. Hell, it never hurts to do your fellow man a good turn when you can.

The other one said, "My name is Childress. I'm with the *Houston Post*. Reports say that it was you and your gang that pulled off the robbery of the transfer agent taking money to the Cotton Exchange about two months ago in Houston. Is this true?"

I looked at him. I said, "I never been in Houston in my life. And from what I hear ain't nobody in his right mind ever goes to Houston."

He said, "And you didn't rob that money?"

I said, "Get it straight. I never robbed nobody in my life."

Behind the two at the bars of my cell was the third man. He had some kind of apparatus on a tripod that he was busy setting up. It took me a minute but then I recognized it as a camera. I said, "What the hell is that sonofabitch doing?" I pointed at him with my cigarillo.

This Bailey said, "Well, Mr. Young, he's going to take your picture. If you don't mind."

I said, "Hell yes, I mind!" The sheriff was kind of off to their left and to the back. I said, "Sheriff Langley, this man ain't going to take my picture! Get them out of here."

He said, "Aw, Wilson, now one little picture ain't going to hurt. Cm'on now, don't be hardheaded about this."

I got off my bunk and said, "I'm telling you, ain't nobody taking my picture!"

But they'd kind of fallen away so that the man with the camera was facing me. I said, "I'm telling you!"

But I seen they weren't going to listen to me so I just turned on my heel and walked to the back of the cell. Just as I did the illuminating powder went off. But all he was going to get was a picture of my back.

Facing the wall I said, "Now, sheriff, I've put up with all this bullshit I'm going to put up with. You get them folks out of here. I don't mind talking with them, but I ain't going to have my picture took!"

Behind me I could hear them talking amongst themselves. I heard the sheriff say, in a kind of high-pitched voice, "Well, you can see how he is. Now if ya'll will just gentle down and get that camera out of here, I reckon he'll come on back and visit with ya'll a bit more."

One of them said, "Will he admit to being Wilson Young?"

I could almost imagine the sheriff making that little head duck before he said, "Well, now that I don't know. That's up to him."

And then the other one said, "I want to ask him a few more questions. Will he turn around if the camera is out of here?"

I said, "Yeah, I will. If they ain't too damn foolish a questions."

I heard them whispering among themselves and then the sheriff said, "Wilson, the cameraman is gone."

I said, "I didn't hear that door going into the office shut."

They whispered some more and then I heard this one say, "Well, you better go on. Take your camera and go on out there and wait for us. Maybe we can talk him into it later."

I waited until I heard the outer door open and shut. Then I looked around kind of careful. It was just the two newspaper reporters and the sheriff. I turned all the way around and walked over and got me some more brandy and water and then went and sat down on my bunk. Then I said, "All right. What can I do for you gentlemen."

The one called Childress, from the *Houston Post*, said, "Sir, is it true you've killed seventeen men? Or how many have you killed, by your own count?"

Well, I'd already figured the man was a fool, being from where he was, but I hated to keep shaming him about it. I said, in a kind of a friendly voice, "Well, I've killed two already this morning. And you keep on with this kind of bullshit you're liable to be the third." I looked at the sheriff. "That's enough of this, Tom. Get these gentlemen out of here. I'll be glad to talk with them when they ain't drunk."

Then I went and sat down on my bunk. The sheriff said, "Well, Wilson, won't you say anything else to them? They could be good friends of yours if you'd let them."

I looked up. "Yeah, I'll say this. I don't belong in

this jail cell. I never done nobody no harm that didn't have it coming to them. In fact I reckon I've done less harm to most folks than anybody I know."

The reporter Bailey said, "Is that a quote from Wilson Young?"

I looked at the sheriff. "Tom, get them out of here for right now. Maybe I'll talk to them later."

He went to herding them out and I'll be goddam if they both didn't touch their hands to them silly little straw skimmers they was wearing and say, "Thank you, Mr. Young."

I heard them go out and I sat there drinking whiskey and water and smoking. After a time the sheriff came back in. He had his hat off and was mopping his brow with a bandana. He leaned up against the bars and said, "Well, Wilson, I appreciate you talking to them. I can't say you done the best as of could of been done. But then you didn't do me that much harm neither."

I said, "Well, I'm glad of that."

He looked around the cell. "You doing all right in there?"

I gave him a face. "Oh, hell, yes. I feel right at home."

"When you going to be ready for some supper?"

I said, "Every time one of ya'll comes back here you want to know if I'm ready to eat something. What are ya'll trying to do—fatten me up for the kill?"

Well, that made him laugh, though I didn't see no humor in it. He said, "Naw, we jest want you to be content. Man like you might be hard to hold if he ain't content." And then he give me a big wink.

I said, "Then send over to Nuevo Laredo for me a woman. That's what makes me content."

And I swear to God, the big fool wrinkled up his brow like he was considering it. He said, "Well, I don't know. We might could handle something like that a little later. But I don't reckon right now, Wilson."

I damn near laughed. But I said, with a straight face, "That's all right. I'm a married man anyway."

He brightened up at that. He said, "Are you now? I'd of never took you fer such. Where's the little woman? You want us to get word to her?"

I said, "Oh, she'll hear."

He pushed back from the bars. "Well, you holler when you're ready for supper." He started out and then stopped. "You know them newspaper boys didn't no more believe you ain't Wilson Young than I do."

I said, "Maybe I'll go to law about them too, if they write something I don't like."

The balance of the day passed as slowly as any time I could remember. I put off ordering supper just as long as I could so as to have something to look forward to. Which is a hell of a commentary on the sorry state my life had reached. Finally, some time after dark, I sent over for some fried chicken and vegetables. Claude brought it in, a big tray covered with a napkin. Surprisingly enough, he didn't have his shotgun bearing backup with him. But he did make me stay away from the cell door while he set my tray in the little window. I said to him, "Where's your running mate, Claude? Or have you figured out I ain't all that dangerous, locked up and unarmed?"

He said, "Aw, don't hoorah me, Mr. Young."

I said, "You better look out, I'm liable to spit and kill you dead."

I noticed he always wore the ring of keys looped

over the butt of his side gun. It looked kind of careless to me, but naturally, I didn't give him the benefit of my thinking.

Before he left I asked him about the old man I'd noticed in the end cell when they'd first brought me in. Claude just shook his head. "That old man is crazy. Must be over sixty and still thinks he is a desperado. Do you know what that old man tried? He tried to rob the mail wagon on the road to San Antonio. Blame fool was damn lucky that he didn't get his head blowed off. Driver and the guard taken his gun away from him and tied him hand and foot and brung him in to us."

I had to laugh. "Goddam, tried it single-handed?"

"Single-handed! At his age. And do you know his damn old pistol wouldn't even fire? Damn firing pin was bent." He shook his head. "Shur'ff ain't the slightest idee what to do with him. Hates to turn him loose fer fear he'll do it again. But prison'll kill him sure as shootin'."

"Maybe he'll promise to behave if you give him a good talking to. I know I would."

He give me a look like he wasn't sure if I was serious or not. But he said, "Damned old fool don't know that times is changin'. He don't know they ain't no room fer his kind no more."

"Or mine," I said. "Or I mean who you think I am. This Wilson Young."

He said, "Aw, now, Mr. Young, I never meant you. They's lots of folks still thinks you is the cat's meow."

I said, "Then turn me loose so I can go on helpin' them enjoy life."

He give me a wink, or what passed for one, and said: "Naw, this is a bunch better. This way we got you where you can be inspected without no danger to the one wanting to see."

I just gave him a tight smile and didn't say anything. His words were only too goddam true.

I ate and then just sat and smoked and drank brandy and tried not to think too much. Every so often one of the deputies would come back to check on me, but we never passed no words. When I finally thought there was a chance I could sleep I lay down on my bunk and put my arm over my eyes to shut out the light from the lantern they kept burning all night.

But of course I couldn't sleep. I was able to keep myself from thinking of Marianne and my partners and my own sorry plight, however, by dwelling on other things. I thought of the three boys that had done me such harm, first trying to rob me and then pointing me out to the sheriff. Well, that had been mostly my fault, as Wilcey would be quick to point out. I needn't have told them my name. But a past mistake is a past mistake and, just like a dead horse, won't get you anywhere no matter how hard you whip it.

I wondered if they might have run into a little misfortune themselves by now. I remembered the bare nod Chulo had made into the cafe. He couldn't have meant anyone except those boys. To tell you the truth I didn't much care what he did to them. Not that it mattered. Where I was at I couldn't do anything about it one way or the other. And if he didn't deal with them, I wasn't sure, once I was free, that I wouldn't.

One little mistake. Just one little mistake was all it took in my profession. And nothing brought it more plainly to mind than the one I'd made.

Well, the robbery of the boat had been a damn good

idea. And it would have worked. The whole plan would have worked. But I hated to think of that, for thinking about the robbery, and its purpose, only led to Marianne; to Marianne and the safe, pleasant life we could have lived together for a long time.

That, more than anything, put the rusty knife of anguish through me. I was just starting to have something to live for, something I'd wanted all my life.

And then to have it jerked away so swiftly and cruelly.

Ah, how easy it was to make plans. And the plans had looked so good. I had worked them out so carefully in my mind, down to the last detail. Except I hadn't counted on bars, the steel bars that made all my well-laid plans suddenly go a-glimmering.

I resolutely shut my mind off from what might have been. Tomorrow was going to be the time to start figuring out how I was going to get out of jail. I still didn't know how, but I knew I'd do it.

I forced myself to relax and then I guess I was tireder than I'd thought, for I went rapidly to sleep.

Of course when I awoke the next morning it took me a second or two to recognize my surroundings and then despair set in. But I would not let it; I fought my spirits back up. Despairing was not going to feed the bear, and if you don't feed the bear, the bear will eat you for lack of something better.

They brought me coffee, unbidden, and a wash basin full of water and some soap. I rinsed my mouth out as best I could and used the wash cloth they'd furnished to scrub at my teeth. After that I laced up a cup of coffee with brandy and sipped at that and smoked a cigarillo. I figured I was going to get a lot of smoking and drinking done before I got out of their goddam jail.

I was just sitting there, trying to start thinking about my plight when I heard a voice hailing me from the other end of the cells. "Hey, there! Hey there, Wilson Young! Hey!"

It was the old man, or at least that's who it sounded like with his cracked old voice.

I walked over to the bars. Naturally, I couldn't see him, but I could tell the voice was coming from the end cell. I said, "I ain't Wilson Young, but if it's me you're hollering at, what do you want?"

He said, "How you liken jail?"

I said, "About as well as I'd enjoy a broken back."

He cackled at that, an old man's laugh. He said, "I been in plenty of 'em. This'un's better'n most. I taken note they treatin' you jest fine."

I said, "I got the money to pay for it."

He cackled again. "I ain't. So I'm eatin' jail house food. Don't ker though. Teeth is near gone and kain't chew much besides mush so it all tastes about one fer me."

I told him I was sorry to hear that. Then I said, "They tell me you tried to hold up a mail coach single-handed. Ain't that a kind of risky business?"

He snorted. "Starvin' to death is what is risky business. Man get's hungry enough he'll try anything."

"Was you that hungry?"

"Hell yes! I been in the outlaw trade, man and boy, fer better'n forty years. You don't reckon I'd be sech a chucklehead as to try a play like'n thet iffen I wasn't desperate."

Well, he had a good point there. The old man wasn't as crazy as Claude thought he was.

About then the corridor door opened and the chief deputy come through. He stopped at the old man's cell. "Billy, now dammit, cut out the hollerin'. We can hear you clean across the street."

Then he came on back to me and asked if I wanted breakfast. I ordered up a big mess of scrambled eggs. "And any kind of side meat they got. Ham or bacon or whatever." He'd stopped a few feet away, for I was at the cell door. I waved him to come closer, but he said, "Just go on back to your cot, Mr. Young."

"Oh, hell," I said, but I done like he told me. When he was at the cell door, I jerked my head in the old man's direction and said, "And bring him the same thing. Might leave off the side meat. Tells me he can't chew. And bring us both plenty of coffee. That jail house coffee of yours ain't the best I ever tasted."

He looked about half disgusted. "Well, it's your money if you want to waste it on that old fool. He wouldn't know the difference of bad to good."

I said, "I'll even waste some more. You had your breakfast yet?"

"Well, no," he said. "Now that you ask it."

I said, "Well, take enough out of my money and have it on me. And don't be in no rush bringing ours back. Take time to eat yours."

Well, he got a kind of surprised smile on his big, ugly face. He said, "Why that's mighty neighborly of you, Mr. Young."

I said, "That's about all I can do in here—be neighborly."

After he'd left Billy called out to me again. He said,

"I don't reckon you know this, Mr. Young, but you kilt my brother. Or so I heerd."

I didn't know what to say for a second and then I said: "Well, to begin with, I ain't Wilson Young. And I know I never killed your brother because I ain't never killed nobody."

He kind of cackled. "I don't blame you. But they going to prove you Wilson Young bye and bye. But hold on to it as long as you can." He paused and then said, "Naw, I doubt if you even recollect it. But my brother was Tom White. I'm Billy White and we was both in the outlaw trade, but they used to call my brother Kid Blanco. Kid White. I heerd he was tryin' to horn in on a bank robbery you was tryin' to pull down in Uvalde and he just kep' on and kep' on until you had to shoot him to get shet of him." He paused. "Kain't say as I blame you, knowin' my brother as I did."

It come back like a flood. So many years ago. I tried to think. That was the robbery that had gone so wrong, where Chico, Harlan Thomas' partner, had been killed and Tod Richter, Les' cousin. But it hadn't been me that had killed the old man; it had been that worthless Harlan Thomas. The old man had followed Tod Richter out to our camp outside of Uvalde. He'd been an old man in his fifties, over the hill, but still wanting one last chance. I'd told him we couldn't use him, to ride on, but it was no use. He'd kept on persisting. Finally, he was going to show me how fast he was. And when he'd reached for his gun, Harlan Thomas had shot him.

For no good reason. The old man hadn't been any threat to us. He'd reminded me of an old retriever dog that Tod and Les and I had kind of shared when we were growing up. He'd got so used to going out on the lake with us in the boat that we could never get rid of him when we were going fishing. If we didn't let him in the boat, he'd swim out and try and get in. Finally, one day, Tod had just up and shot him.

But, then, Tod had been about as worthless as Harlan Thomas.

Harlan Thomas had never lived long to enjoy his gun work, for I'd killed him the next day when he'd tried to run out on us after we'd been run to ground by the posse that was chasing us and had to fort up.

The old man called again. "You recollect killing my brother? Kid Blanco?"

I said, "No, Billy, I never killed your brother. You have my word on that."

Not long after that Claude came back with our breakfasts. I could hear Billy down at the end of the corridor saying to Claude, "What's this? This for me?" Then I heard Claude tell him I'd bought it and he said: "Well, goddam, that's a gentleman for you. You betcha he's Wilson Young. Ain't no small timers would do a trick like this."

I smiled sourly to myself. Convicted by buying breakfast. Hell, a man just can't be too careful.

Which is what Claude said when he brought my breakfast down. After I'd taken the tray and was sitting on my cot eating, he kept standing there, giving me what he probably thought was a shrewd look. He said, "You know old Billy, crazy as he is, just damn shore laid his finger on somethin' I'd been thinkin' on my own self. He said wasn't no small timers bought breakfast. And ain't no cattle buyers from Matagorda County does neither. Man goes around buyin' breakfast fer two other fellers he don't hardly know, why he don't have to work too hard fer his money. Gets it easy, if you know what I mean."

I said, "I know some cattle buyers might take offense at what you just said about them being cheap."

"Oh, that ain't all of it. I noticed somethin' else." He cocked his head to one side and eyed me hard. "You ain't mad enough for a man thet's been falsely arrested. Iffen we really had a cattle buyer in here instead of Wilson Young, you'd be yelling your head off and sendin' fer ever' lawyer in town. Shur'ff done took note of that."

I just went on eating. Then I said, "You and the sheriff are just too damn smart for me. I ain't got a chance. Whyn't ya'll just take me on out and hang me now and be done with it."

He looked shocked. "Oh, they won't hang you! Hang Wilson Young? Hell, I reckon not! Me and the shur'ff wouldn't stand for it."

I said, "Well, if you get word that's in their plans, let me know." I took another bite and then said, "Oh, by the way, how you know I haven't already sent for my lawyer?"

"Huh? Naw, you haven't. You'd of had to ast me or the shur'ff and you ain't done it."

"How do you know I didn't figure to send for him through them newspaper people. What they wrote. My lawyer reads the newspaper, you know."

Well, he didn't know exactly what to say to that. I added, "And me and the sheriff made a deal. You say I ain't mad enough. What's the good of me getting mad and causing myself a lot of trouble. Ya'll ain't going to let me out just because I get mad. And if I get mad and cause a hell of a ruckus, I ain't going to be allowed to send out for my meals or to have whiskey and smokes." Now I gave him the eye. "You think on that. But like I say, you and the sheriff are just too smart for me."

Well, it sent him off mumbling to himself. I'd knocked down this entire edifice he'd had built up in his head.

Only thing was, maybe they were too smart for me. After all, it was me that was behind the bars.

The sheriff came back not too long after I'd finished breakfast. He looked like a busy man. He didn't seem to be as afraid to come near my cell as Claude was. He even got right up to the door while I was standing on the other side. After we'd made a little small talk he said, "Well, Mr. Young, I done had a wire from the law in Houston. They want to send one of them guards up here to see if he can't identify you as the man who robbed that transfer money that was headed for the Cotton Exchange. Seems that reporter that was here yestiday wired back and they done got themselves all hot and bothered about it. What do you think of that."

I said, "That sounds mighty good to me, sheriff. I'll be glad to see all the witnesses you can roust up to get here so we can get this misunderstanding cleared up and I can be on my way."

He looked kind of disappointed. He said, "Well, I just wanted you to know."

I said, "That's damn good of you."

He hesitated, as if trying to decide how he wanted to say something. Then he said, "Listen, they's liable to be a hell of a jurisdiction fight over you. I figure this

THE TEXAS BANK ROBBING COMPANY

county's got first claim cause we ketched you. But soon's the word gets out I figure all hell's going to break loose and every county in this state is going to try to make a claim to try you. But I want you to know we going to do everything in our pow'r to hold on to you."

I just looked at him. Wasn't much I could say to that.

The morning passed so slowly I almost got to thinking it was time for the sun to go down. I looked at the window a lot, but I still hadn't let myself go to it and pull up and look at the outside world. I was afraid it would be too much and cause that panic to set in again.

Billy and I visited some. But there wasn't a lot we could talk about. He wanted to cut up old touches about the jobs we'd both pulled, but since I wasn't about to talk about such things at the top of my voice, it kind of put a damper on the conversation.

The noon meal came and went. I drank a little whiskey and smoked a hell of a lot of cigarillos.

In the middle of the afternoon I was laying on my cot, about half dozing, when I heard the outer door open. I took my arm off from my face and seen the sheriff coming down the corridor. He stopped in front of my cell. "Wilson," he said. "I got some mighty good news for you."

"Yeah?" I swung my legs around and sat up. "What kind of news."

He said, "You want to borrow my razor and soap? Get yourself kind of slicked up?"

I said, "What the hell are you talking about?"

"Your old lady is here. Your wife. She's come to see you."

I just stared at him. Finally I said, "What are you talking about? Where the hell did she come from?"

He said, "Well, you ought to know that better'n I do. But she's here." Then he gave a low whistle. "And boy is she a looker. Which don't surprise me none, seeing as how you are who you are."

I said, "You mean she's here? In this jail?"

He jerked a thumb. "Right out there. Right in the office. Sittin' right out there in a chair across from my desk. And ever' goddam deputy I got standin' around with his tongue hangin' out."

"Oh, shit!" I said slowly. "I didn't want her comin' here, seeing me like this. Locked up."

He give me an understanding look. "I can see what you mean, ol' hoss. But there it is. She's here. So what are you going to do about it? You want that razor and soap? I can stall her that long."

I shook my head, slowly. "No, I reckon not. But this has kind of taken me unawares." Then I suddenly looked up at him. "Listen, sheriff, and listen close to me. You don't want no trouble off me. But I tell you this, you involve her in this mess in any way and I'll be more trouble than your daddy gave you. You understand me?"

"Well, hell, Wilson," he said, "I ain't never been gonna cause her no trouble. I wouldn't have caused you nar'en if it hadn't of been my job. She ain't got nothin' to do with this. Bein' married to an outlaw ain't no crime, you know."

But all I could think of was that shotgun messenger coming down to identify me. And if he saw her he'd identify her as well. That just gave me a sick feeling in the bottom of my stomach.

THE TEXAS BANK ROBBING COMPANY

The sheriff said, "Well, you ready for her to come on back?"

I took a deep breath. I had to talk to her, tell her to get out of town. I said, "Yeah, I reckon."

He looked at me. "Well, at least you ought to take your fingers and kind of slick your hair back a little. Won't hurt to let her see you're makin' the best of a bad bargain."

I said, "Yeah, yeah. Go ahead. Send her on back."

He said, "I'll send her back with Claude. I got to get out and kind of circulate around town." Then he gave me another one of them things that I figured he thought passed for a wink. "I got to get all the mileage I can out of you, hoss."

"Good luck," I said.

After he'd gone I poured me out a big drink of brandy and took it down straight. All I knew to tell her and to make her understand was that she had to get out of town. To get as far away from what was fixing to happen as possible. The idea that she might get caught in the same net with me was just more than I could bear. I had to make her understand she had to leave me, get on a train and leave. Get word back to me where she was, but she had to get out of Laredo.

I heard the outer door open. I went to the cell door, straining to see down the corridor. After a little she came into my vision and my heart damn near went out of me.

Chapter Seven

Well, she was still as beautiful as she was the last time I'd seen her, which was hard to believe had only been the previous day. So bad had I missed her that it had seemed we'd been separated a year.

She kind of smiled and shook her head as soon as she saw me, shook her head as if to say, "Now what kind of trouble have you got yourself in?" She was wearing the light blue ankle-length dress that I liked so much and she looked very ladylike with a little blue hat perched on her blond hair. Claude was coming right behind her, carrying a shotgun and looking mighty important.

Before she could speak I held up my hand. "Don't say anything yet." Then I said to the deputy, "Claude, now you get on out of here. This is a private conversation between me and my wife."

He stopped, but he said, "Now, Mr. Young, you

know I got to be in here. You ain't allowed to see nobody by yourself except your lawyer."

I said, "Quit calling me Mr. Young. How many times I got to tell you my name is Wilson. Jim Wilson." But I said that for Marianne's benefit, to let her know I wasn't admitting to being Wilson Young. Then I said, "Listen, what the hell you think she's carrying? A cannon? You searched her purse, didn't you?"

"Well, yes."

"Then you got to know she ain't trying to smuggle nothing in to me."

"Yeah, but we didn't look under her dress."

I looked at him for a long half minute. Then I said, "Claude it's just such remarks as that will get you killed if I was to get out of here."

He kind of flinched back a little. He said, hurriedly, "Now, Mr. Young, I didn't mean nothin' by that. Alls I meant was we couldn't give her a all-out search, she being a lady. So I got to stay in here and watch ya'll. The shur'ff would have my hide if I didn't."

I finally said, "Well, all right. But you get back up there at the end, up there by the door. And you watch, but you damn well better not try to listen!"

He went backing up to the door. "All right, I'm a-goin'. I ain't wantin' to interfere with a private conversation between a man an' his wife. But if you could ask the lady to keep her hands where I kin see 'em."

"Just get on back there."

Then I turned to Marianne. She'd been standing there, right in front of me, waiting for me to finish with Claude. Without a word she leaned over and we kissed through the bars. It wasn't a real good kiss, but it was as good as we could do under the circumstances.

Then she looked at me and shook her head. "I swear—I can't let you out of my sight for five minutes without you getting into trouble."

I ran my hand through my hair kind of ruefully. "Seems like it, don't it. Well, I will say I been places I liked better." We were talking low, but then I whispered, "By the way, I ain't admitting to being Wilson Young. I been telling them my name is Jim Wilson."

"I know," she said. She had a newspaper under her arm and she got it out and opened it. The headline read: WILSON YOUNG DENIES BEING WILSON YOUNG.

Well, that give us both a pretty good laugh. She passed the newspaper through the bars and I took it and pitched it over on my cot.

Then she gave me a serious look. Our heads were very close together and we were speaking in a low whisper to make sure Claude couldn't hear. She said, "Oh, Will, this is so awful. Are you able to stand it?"

I shrugged. "I guess I got to. I don't seem to have no selection on the matter."

She just shook her head. "God, what damn bad luck! Just when we had everything figured out."

I said quickly, "No, no. None of that. I can't afford to think like that right now or I would go crazy."

She got even closer to the bars. "Listen, we're going to get you out. And very quickly."

"Who's going to get me out? You're going to get on a train and get the hell out of Laredo."

She drew herself up a little. "Oh, no I'm not. I knew you'd start that old stuff and there's no way I'm going to leave. Not as long as you're in this jail."

I said, "Marianne, please don't worry me about this. Look, I'd feel a whole lot easier in my mind if I knew you were safe in Arkansas or St. Louis or some such place. God, it's bad enough for you to see me in here, locked up like some damn animal. I can't stand to think of you out there by yourself in this damn hole."

She said, "Will, don't ask me to do it. I won't. I couldn't stand to be off somewhere else with you locked up in this goddam jail. You've got to let me stay until this is all over. Besides, I'm not by myself. I've got Chulo and Wilcey to look after me."

I shrugged. What could I say. If the truth be told, I didn't want her to go away. Not really. I said, "How are they doing?"

"They're worried, just like I am. But, Will—we're going to get you out of here. Wilcey and Chulo are ready to do anything. And—" She hesitated. "And Austin Davis is going to help us."

I kind of jerked my head back. "The hell he is! No way!"

"Yes, Will, yes. Now please listen." She was whispering very rapidly, for I'm sure she'd predicted my reaction in advance. She said, "Chulo and Wilcey ain't smart enough to pull off something like this and you say yourself that Wilcey is not that good with a gun. And you've told me that Austin Davis is smart and smooth. He came forward this morning and volunteered to help and we're going to let him."

I looked at her. "Yeah, and what's the price?"

She said, "Oh, Will, don't think like that. You'll drive yourself crazy if you go to thinking like that. Listen, absolutely nothing is going to happen with Austin Davis and me. It makes me feel like a fool to even have to tell you that."

I said, "You don't know what a lady killer he is."

She said, in a fierce whisper, "Goddammit, Wilson, I am not a child. You know I didn't come riding into town on a load of cotton fresh off the farm. I can handle any man and I happen to belong to you."

I looked down at the cell floor. "I guess," I said. "I'm just not thinking real straight right now."

"You certainly aren't. Austin Davis has been a perfect gentleman. Chulo and Wilcey brought him up to our room and he badly wants to help. He wants to be your friend. He admires you. He wants to ride with you, and if he can help get you out of jail, I think you ought to let him."

I kind of half smiled at that. "Hell, I'd let the devil himself ride with me if he'd get me out of this cage."

She said, "We're going to get you out, honey. Don't you worry."

"Any plans yet?"

She shook her head. "No. Chulo and Austin and Wilcey are talking it over right now. I was supposed to come over here and see you and let you know that we're working on it. And I don't want you to worry, honey. This damn hick jail can't hold you."

Well, I was feeling considerably better, just seeing her. And it made me feel all the more so knowing my partners weren't going to let me down. We talked on for a little while longer and then Claude called out, "Mr. Young, I got to ask your little lady to leave. I got other work and I can't stay in here the balance of the day. She can come back this afternoon if she wants to."

I said, "All right, Claude." He came down the corridor a little way and I give him a hard look. I said, "Claude, you weren't listening to anything we were saying, were you? You didn't hear anything, did you?"

He shook his head. "No sir."

I said, "How do you know?"

"How do I know what?"

"How do you know you didn't hear anything we were saying. You said you weren't listening. You'd of had to have been listening to know you didn't hear anything."

He said, "Well, I—" Then he stopped and gave me a puzzled look. "Mr. Young, that don't make any sense. I mean I—"

But Marianne and I were laughing.

When she was gone, I settled back on my bunk and just kind of sat there, smoking and drinking brandy and water and feeling considerably better about the situation. Damn straight I was still in jail, but there now seemed a chance I might get out sooner than I'd thought. The people that were holding me were just men; the people who were trying to get me out were men also.

I figured my people were better men than the people holding me.

Thinking on that I looked up at that barred window. The outside didn't seem so faraway as it had. I took another drag off my cigarillo, flipped it away, and then walked up to the window. I put my hands up slowly and grasped hold of the bars. I began to pull with the strength in my shoulders and my upper arms. I very slowly raised myself up until my face was in full view of the outside.

It wasn't that wonderful. Twenty yards away, dead ahead, was the side of another building. In between was what looked like a trash heap. Only by canting my head to the side could I see the street that ran out in front of the jail. There I could see a few horsemen passing by, now and again a buggy, and a few foot stragglers.

But I could see the sky and the sunshine. It appeared to be a cloudless day with almost no wind. I could see puffs from the dust in the street raised by the horses' hooves that were passing by. It rose in the air and fell straight back to earth.

I let myself down slowly, thinking about it. It was the outside, it was freedom. And as bad as it looked, it was still what I was going to have and have in a very short time. It was the breath of life to me and I couldn't do without it.

I sat back down on my bunk and picked up the paper Marianne had left for me, laughing just a little over the headline. The main drift of the story was just about as funny. From the story it looked as if they'd caught the original ring-tailed tiger by the tail, right there in Laredo. And if it hadn't of been for Sheriff Langley, none of it would have come to pass.

In the story in the paper, according to Sheriff Langley, they had "apprehended Wilson Young in the Longhorn Cafe after a fierce struggle and managed to disarm the well-known outlaw after he'd resisted arrest with all the power at his means."

Then at the very end, the story said, "The bandit, Wilson Young, claims he is Jim Wilson, a cattle buyer from somewhere down on the coast."

The last thing in the piece was another remark by Sheriff Langley where he said: "This should be a stern warning to other bandits like Wilson Young that we ain't going to put up with them coming down to Webb County and trying to pull their depredations."

After I put the paper down I went to yelling for a deputy to come. From down the way Billy White said, "What's wrong, Mr. Young?"

I said, "Never mind, old man. I've just got me some satisfaction to get."

Finally a deputy come back, not Claude, and wanted to know what was the matter. I said, "Get the sheriff up here. I got something I want to show him."

The deputy said, "I think he's busy."

"Well, tell him to come as soon as he can."

I sat there smoking and drinking brandy until the corridor door opened and Sheriff Langley appeared. He came up to my cell door and leaned against the bars. "Somethin' I kin do for you, Wilson?"

"Yeah," I said. I took the newspaper and read him the part about where I'd been apprehended and disarmed only after I'd resisted arrest with all the power at my means. Then I looked up at the sheriff. He was looking a little embarrassed. I said, "You kind of put on the dog a little there, didn't you, sheriff?"

He fidgeted around a little. "Well, you know them newspaper boys. They got to stretch anything you tell them."

"Sure," I said. "It was all their doing. No doubt about it."

He said, "Well, maybe I made it sound a little bit worse than what it really was."

I said, "Yes, considering you had a double-barreled shotgun pressed up against the back of my head, I'd say you did gild the lily just a little. But I reckon it's all in a day's work of getting votes."

He grinned kind of sheepishly. "I'm an old man,

Wilson. I need that one more term. A man's got to get his living."

"Well, that's all this Wilson Young has been trying to do, get his living. And you want to put him in jail."

He said, "Well, ever'body's got they job. Yours and mine just have to get at loggerheads. And when you going to quit denying you're Wilson Young?"

"I ain't ever going to quit denying it. Because I ain't."

"Ah, pshaw, Wilson. That old dog won't hunt. I done wired off for a half dozen witnesses. Man, you can't be as well known as you are and expect to deny your name."

"Where'd you wire to?"

"Aw, different places. Houston, mostly. El Paso. Uvalde. Few places where you pulled robberies. Couldn't wire them all. The county would have gone broke paying for the telegrams." Then a frown flickered over his face. "I'm a little sorry I wired the law in Houston. They so hot and bothered about that bank messenger you robbed down there that I'm afeared they going to give us a jurs'diction fight over the matter. I done had two wires today from the sheriff down there and he means to claim yore body." The sheriff was chewing tobacco and he took time to spit on the floor and then shift his cud from one cheek to another. "But I tell you—I don't plan to give you up to nobody. Yore trial ought to be a humdinger. An' I intend on seein' it's held right here in Laredo."

I said, "Hell, that ought to get you enough votes to run for mayor."

He said, "You might not be half wrong."

After he was gone I lay on my bunk and stared up

at the ceiling. My main thoughts were centered around the fact that it might not be all that easy to make my escape from the jail. And if they were to succeed in getting me down to someplace like Houston, I really might have a hell of a time. It could be that my next stop might be the state prison. I'd seen it from a distance once when I was passing through Huntsville. The Walls, they called it. The very sight had made me shudder. The whole place was surrounded by brick walls fifteen feet high with a guard tower at every corner. They got a man in a place like that he might as well give his heart to God because his ass was damn sure going to belong to his captors.

I had felt good right after Marianne came, but as the day waned the worried doubts came back to my mind. Mostly I just lay on my cot and smoked and drank and thought. Not that there was that much to think about; I just kept worrying the situation over and over in my mind. I had no idea what plans my partners and Marianne and Austin Davis could come up with, and the more I thought about it, the more I doubted they could come up with an idea that would see me free. That sheriff had the same as told me he wasn't taking any chances on losing me, not to freedom and not to any other law.

I just flat couldn't see what they were going to do to get me out.

I ate a late meal and then spent most of the afternoon pacing back and forth in my cell. Marianne did not come back to visit me, nor did anyone else. I'd about halfway expected the newspaper boys would be back, though I didn't see where they needed to talk to me. They could make it up better than I could tell it.

It was a long day and night. From time to time one of the deputies would come back to check on me, but other than the few words I exchanged with them and the few shouted conversations I had with Billy White, there wasn't a damn thing to make the time pass any faster.

I read the paper from cover to cover, which was quite a feat, considering the quality of the publication. I actually took more enjoyment out of reading the walls of my cell. Prisoners long gone before me had inscribed their passing with knife and pencil on the walls, leaving a record of their names and their woeful plight. They said things like: "Juan Garcian, 1894. A poor Mexican far from home." And "George Holmes, June, 1891. They said I done it, but I never did. And now they'll be putting me away for a long time."

That one made me shudder a little. I'd done it, but that didn't make it any easier to think of being put away for a long time.

One said: "Jim Decker, Robstown, Texas. I wish I'd of stayed at home." Another: "Boyd Fisher. At 17 years of age I have ruint my life from drink and a foolish misdeed."

There was one long one, awkwardly scrawled in pencil. It said: "I am Jack Knox of Newton County. They are hanging me in the morning. If anybody that reads this ever gets to Wichita Falls, tell Sally I done it fer her. Though I don't reckon she'll ever see a penny of the money as they done caught me too quick."

No, I reckon Sally never did see a penny of the money. Though that was just about the story of a man. Seems that a man did everything he did for a woman, including robbing and stealing. Only sometimes the price got a little too high, something this Jack Knox must have thought of just before they sprung the door to drop him down at the end of a rope.

Well, I couldn't say I'd taken up robbing and killing as a result of any one woman. I'd just done it because there was no other way to get what I needed to be a success in life.

Some success, I thought—in a jail cell facing God knows what kind of future.

But that was my story. And I didn't reckon I was alone in my foolishness. Most men went at life like a fool a-fucking, without fear or forethought.

It got dark and I tried to walk myself down so that I'd be able to sleep, but it was a hard job, as afire with worry as my brain was. Finally, I took several good stiff drinks and then lay down and shut my eyes, determined to sleep.

But it was a long time and many anxious thoughts later before I did finally succeed in drifting off.

Next morning I bought breakfast for myself and Claude and Billy. Claude acted like no one had ever done him a good turn before. But he did say, "Mr. Young, now I don't want you doin' this no more after taday. You only got just so much money in there an' ain't no use you spendin' it up on me and Billy White." Then he asked, "Is yore whiskey holdin' out arright? Need me to fetch you some more yet?"

I shook my head. "No, not yet. I'll let you know." To tell you the truth I wanted to send somebody else who might come back with a little better quality. I didn't figure old Claude knew much more about buying whiskey other than getting what was the cheapest. And figuring he was doing me a favor in the bargain.

When the food came I dawdled over breakfast, dreading to face another long day with nothing to do except sit and smoke and drink and think. But then, almost before I was through, Sheriff Langley came back and said, "Well, he's here."

It put a bolt of fright through me for a second. I figured he was talking about some lawman from Houston who'd come to pick me up and transport me back to that big city jail in Houston from which, I felt sure, there'd be no escape. So, with sinking heart, I said, "Who? Who's here?"

"Why your lawyer." He gave me a kind of reproachful look. "You know you might have done better gettin' one of the local boys. They'd of appreciated it and worked mighty hard for you. And it'd of done me some good with them too."

I said, "What the hell are you talking about?"

He said, "Why your damn out-of-town lawyer. One from where you say you live. Matagorda County. The one you sent for. Jim Davis he said his name was. Said he read in the paper up yonder what had done happened to you and got here jest quick's he could."

"Oh," I said.

He looked. "You 'bout through with yore breakfast anyway. Soon's we get him searched I'll have him brought on back." He looked at me a moment more. "He looks like kind of a dandy. Is he a good one?"

"Good what?"

"Lawyer."

"Oh, hell yes," I said. "Good's they come."

The sheriff left and I sat there wondering who in the hell was coming through the door representing himself

THE TEXAS BANK ROBBING COMPANY

as my lawyer. Well, it didn't matter. I was going to be glad to see anyone, lawyer or not.

I finished my breakfast and then added some more brandy to my coffee cup and sat back to see what the situation would bring. Then the door opened and Claude brought my "lawyer" back. It was Austin Davis, though I'd of hardly recognized him. He was got up in a sack suit and vest with a four-in-hand tie and was wearing a little derby on his head and carrying a carpetbag. If I hadn't of known better I'd of took him for a lawyer, for he looked as much like one as the real article. He came straight up to the cell and said, "I got here as quick as I could, Mr. Wilson, as soon as I heard the news. Just rest your mind. I'm here to get you out of this mess just as quick as it can be done."

Claude came up behind him then, carrying a shotgun, and Austin Davis said, "Unlock this cell and let me in."

Claude said, "That makes me nervous. And the sheriff don't like it neither."

Davis said, "Now, listen, we done argued this out in the office. You know you got to let me have time alone with Mr. Wilson. That's the law. A man is entitled to a private conversation with his lawyer."

Claude rubbed his chin. "Goddammit, why can't you just talk to him from out here."

"Because it ain't the way it's supposed to be. Now ya'll have searched me stem to stern. You even took my pencils. As if they'd make a weapon. You've done made me undress and you've looked through every article of my clothing and you've damn near took my bag apart here. So you just open this cell door and get out of here."

"Oh, hell," Claude said. "Arright. But you make it snappy."

I retreated to the far end of my cot and then Claude unlocked the cell door and let Austin in. He came in and took off the damn silly hat he was wearing and sat down on the other end of my cot. He waited while Claude slammed the cell door shut and locked it. Then he watched while Claude started up the corridor. I could hear the deputy mumbling to himself. Finally, he went on through the office door and Austin said, "Well, Mr. Wilson, I see you've got yourself in a spot of trouble here."

I didn't know how we ought to talk. I didn't know if they could hear or if Billy could hear or just what. So I pointed to my ears before I said anything and looked questioningly. He just shrugged as if he didn't know either. Then he said, "Let's just talk as low as we can. I seen one other prisoner in here, but I don't think he can hear if we whisper real low."

We kind of leaned toward each other and I said, "You sure you want in on this, Austin?"

He shrugged again. "Why not. I was in jail once and I didn't like it. I figure you're liking it even less."

I said, "How's things on the outside? How's Chulo and Wilcey?"

He kind of half smiled. "Well, Wilcey seems convinced they've already hung you and Chulo figures the best way to handle the job is for him just to walk in here and shoot every sonofabitch in sight and then carry you out over his shoulder. I'd say Chulo is getting a little hard to hold."

I said, "There was three boys who identified me. He ain't done nothing to them, has he?" It had been worrying me. Because if he did do something, it wouldn't be no big trick for the law to connect Chulo and Wilcey to me and then we'd all three be in jail. As a matter of fact I was a little surprised they hadn't been recognized.

Austin said, "So far as I know he ain't done nothing to them. But he's *looking* for them. And that ain't good. Right now we don't need no upsets going on."

I said, "You tell him for me that I don't want him to do a damn thing. You tell him if he does I'm going to half kill him. You tell him I mean it. That I'm serious. Chulo's like a mule. You got to hit him square between the eyes with a railroad cross tie just to get his attention. You tell Wilcey that I said they was both to lay low. Just stay the hell out of sight."

He said, "I been trying to tell them that. But they are considerably excited. But maybe they'll listen when I tell them what you had to say."

"You tell them that if they want to see me out of this jail they are to listen to you." Then I added, "And to Marianne. By the way, how's she doing?"

"She ain't happy."

"Neither am I," I said. I looked away and then came back to him and reached under my cot and picked up a bottle of brandy. "You want some of this? Ain't much, but it's all I got."

He said, "Oh, I almost forgot." He opened his little carpetbag and came out with four bottles of good French brandy. He said, "We figured you might be needing this. I was a little surprised the sheriff let me bring this in."

I said, "Oh, it ain't whiskey they are against me

having, it's guns. Won't hear of letting me have a shotgun."

I was mighty grateful for the good brandy, which is the drink I mostly prefer when I can get it. I uncorked a bottle, poured some in my cup, and then said, "Take your pick. The cup or the bottle. I ain't got another cup."

He took the bottle and then we said "luck" and knocked a drink straight back as befits the toast. It was mighty smooth stuff and I said, "Aaaah!"

He reached over and poured my cup full again and then we sat there sipping.

I said, "Well, Marianne tells me you are ramrodding this deal. You got any ideas yet?"

He nodded and took a short pull at the bottle before he said, "Yeah. But it's going to have to be an inside-out job."

"What's that supposed to mean?"

"It means we can't rush this sonofabitch. They is too many men here for that with too many rifles and shotguns. And we can't blow a wall out. Ain't no way to do that without killing you. And we can't wait until they transport you somewhere else. Because if they do it's likely to be some bunch like out of Houston and they will come in force."

"You heard about that?"

He nodded. "It's all over the street." Then he gave me a crooked grin. "You're mighty popular. I'm glad to say I'm pure pleasured I ain't that popular. But just about every county in the state wants the privilege of giving you a party."

I said, "So how is it to be done?"

He said, "The simplest way possible. We've got to get a gun into you so you can let us in."

I laughed sourly. "Think some more. Ain't no way you can get a gun in to me. I doubt if you could even smuggle a bullet in, much less a gun." I jerked my head toward the window at the back of my cell. "See that window? At first I thought somebody could sail me a gun in through those bars. Take a closer look."

He said, "I know. One of the first things I thought of. But there's hog wire on the outside across it. And a deputy checking on it about every fifteen minutes. They got a rope staked off in a circle around it. You can't see it. Strict orders for nobody to get no closer to the side of the jail than that rope."

I hadn't seen the picket rope, but I could imagine. I just said, "So you see? See how they searched you? They seriously don't want me to get out of here. Ain't no way you are going to get a gun in to me."

He said, "I've got a gun on me right now."

I glanced up at him. He wasn't fooling. I said, "Bullshit."

He shook his head. "No, no bullshit. Don't look right at it, but have you ever noticed that big belt buckle I wear?"

Of course I had; you couldn't miss the damn thing. It was about six inches long and about four inches wide and rounded so that it looked as if it weighed a ton. I said, "Yeah, so what?"

He said, "That belt buckle is hollow. It's saved my life more than once. It's where I carry my hideout gun. There's a Derringer in there right now. A .38 caliber Derringer and it's loaded with two cartridges."

I just stared at him. "And they didn't find it?"

He shook his head. "Ain't no way to tell what's inside. It's a very clever little piece. I bought it off a gambler that was down on his luck. It's what I used to break jail in Arkansas when I thought all was up with me."

I said, "Slip it over to me right quick. Just slip it under the blanket."

But he shook his head. "No, ain't the right time. They could search this cell after I leave and then we'd be shit out of luck. I'm coming in the morning and I'll give it to you then. We ain't quite ready for this today."

"When we going to try it?"

"In the morning."

God, words never sounded sweeter to my ears. In the morning. The only thing that would have sounded better would have been, "Right now."

I nodded. "What am I supposed to do?"

He said, "Somehow you've got to get one deputy back here. Would there be any chance he'd have the keys with him?"

I nodded. "Yes. Claude. I can do that. He comes back here to see what I want for breakfast and he's always got the ring of keys looped over the butt of his side gun. He comes alone now." I smiled slowly. "I been buying his breakfast for him."

"What'll he do when you stick that Derringer in his face? Fold up? Yell for help? What? Is he a hero?"

I thought about it for a long moment. Then I said, "He'll fold up and he'll hand me them keys over. Or at least I'm going to bet my life on it. Because the only way he's going to believe that I'll shoot him is if I believe it myself." I looked at Austin Davis. "And I'll

THE TEXAS BANK ROBBING COMPANY

shoot him. I ain't got no other choice. I figure they are going to hang me one way or another. Either at the end of a rope or trying to keep me in a cell. One is just as bad as the other. So he'll know I'm going to shoot him and he'll come to taw."

He nodded. "All right. Then you got to get in that office and get the rest of them deputies covered. Then you crack that front door. Me and Chulo and Wilcey will be sitting our horses right across the street. As soon as I see you crack that front door me and Chulo will be coming in. We'll leave Wilcey out there to watch the front."

"Then what?" I said.

He said, "Then we are coming in and we're going to herd all the law we got caught up in them back cells and just waltz on out the door and head for wherever you think we ought to head for." He paused to take a quick drink of brandy. "What I'm hoping is that we can get as many chicks in the cage as possible. And the sheriff for sure. What time will Claude come back here to see about your breakfast?"

I said, "Judging from the light, just before seven. I don't know if the sheriff is here by that time or not."

He shook his head. "No, he ain't. I watched this morning and he didn't come in until about half past. But that'd be all right too because it's going to take some little time for you to get them folks settled up front, get them disarmed and that front door open, and for us to come in and herd them back and lock them up. We can be watching for the sheriff to come in and put the capture on him just as soon as he walks in the door. He don't look like too much."

"He ain't," I said.

After that we sat a moment, both of us thinking. Just sitting there drinking brandy. Finally I said, "Well, I hope it works. Or, if it don't, I hope I'm the only one gets killed. I hate to think of my partners—" I looked at him. "And you being one, taking this kind of a chance."

He shrugged. "I done worse. Ain't no hill for a stepper." Then he give me that crooked grin. "Hell, I asked if I could work with you in Encinal and you said you'd keep me in your head if something come up. Well, I reckon something did come up."

"Yeah. Damned if it didn't."

He said, "Well, does this suit you? The way I've got it laid out?"

I thought a moment and then I nodded. I said, "Yeah. Austin, the way I've planned all my jobs I've tried to go for as simple a way as possible. You get it too complicated and, considering the people you've got to trust, something is going to get fucked up. You've kept it simple. You've put the gun in the right man's hand. Mine. To tell you the truth—" I looked up at him. "It's about the way I'd of figured it out."

He shrugged. "That ain't bad news to hear."

I said, "All that surprised me is that you are willing to do it. After the way I acted."

He give me that crooked smile again. "I agree with that. I reckon myself to be a damn fool. Don't know anyone else would be this foolish. I ought to leave you in here to rot."

I said, "Aw, go to hell. Quit trying to be so damned nice."

That made him laugh a little bit. He said, "You do look kind of silly in this here cell, Wilson Young."

I give him a look. "You ought to see yourself in that suit you are wearing and that little pork pie hat you got perched on top of your head."

That grin come again. He said, "I don't know, Marianne told me I looked mighty good."

Well, my face went flat and I kind of pulled back. He seen it and threw up his hand and started laughing. "Oh, goddam," he said, "wait a minute! Wait a minute. I see you are in love and I was dead wrong! Now just take it easy. I thought you could handle a little teasing by now, but I see you can't."

I didn't say anything.

He said, "Now, Will. Now, Will. We done had this out. Marianne—"

"Call her my wife."

"All right, all right. Your wife. Your wife never even saw me this morning." He put his hand to his brow. "Goddam, I never saw such a man. You got a blind spot there I wouldn't get in the light of for a free trip to heaven. Damn, you are quick about that."

I didn't say anything.

He said, "I seen Marianne—your wife—last night." He held up a hand. "With Chulo and Wilcey. I laid out what I had in mind. She thought it was all right. Last thing she said to me was that I'd damn well better be right. That I'd better get you out of this hoosegow. Will, that woman belongs to you. Why don't you just kind of take it easy and enjoy it?"

I took a pull of brandy and then I lit a cigarillo. After a moment I said, "Well, I reckon you are right. But locked up in here like I am—worrying like I am."

"I know," he said. "I ought to watch the jokes. But

I know we are going to get you out. And so I can laugh."

Then we heard the runway door open. It was Claude. He yelled, "Now ya'll have had just about long enough! Sheriff wants you out of there!"

Austin got up. He said, "I'll get over here about seven in the morning. I'll get this Derringer in your hands. After that it is up to you."

"Yeah," I said.

"Don't forget to crack the door. We'll be coming in after that."

I said, "Wait a minute."

He was about to turn for the door. I said, "I'm going to trust you with something."

"What?"

I looked down at the cigarillo that was smoking between my fingers. I said, "I want you to get Marianne out of town today. I want you to put her on a train for San Antonio. I want her to go to Chulo's cousin's house. She knows." I looked up at him. "But she ain't going to want to go. I'm going to depend on you to convince her that it will be easier on me if I didn't have to worry about her tomorrow."

He stood there, about half turned toward the cell door, half looking back at me. He said, "You want me to do that?"

"Yes," I said. "She won't listen to Wilcey and she won't listen to Chulo. And I ain't going to have no chance to talk to her. Not before we break out."

From the end of the runway corridor Claude hollered out again, "Now, goddammit, I'm coming back. Lawyer or no lawyer! You got to let me come back there."

Austin said, "Will she go?"

"Tell her if I make it I need her where I can find her. If I don't it won't make any difference anyway. You tell her I understand she wants to be here to see if I make it out of jail. Tell her I understand. But that it won't help me none if I get out and she ain't where I'm going to be looking for her. You tell her to get on that train today and go to Chulo's cousin's house. And tell her I don't mean maybe."

He said, "I gotcha."

From down the hall Claude yelled, "Goddammit, I'm coming back. Lawyer or no lawyer. Shur'ff done told me to."

Austin looked at me. "I appreciate your trust. All I can say is I wisht I had me a woman like you got."

I said, "You just get her on that train."

He nodded. "I'll see to it." He took another step toward the door. Then he turned back and looked at me. He said, "Will, this will go as to however you want it. I guarantee that."

I said, "Aw, get the hell out of here."

Claude yelled again and Austin yelled back. He said, "Then cm'on, goddammit! And quit waking everybody up out there in the front office."

He give me a wink. "See you early tomorrow morning."

"Just get her on that train."

"Don't worry."

I looked at him. I said, "You don't worry me no more. I'll take you to go down the road with."

He never got a chance to say anything, for Claude was coming down the corridor, bustling like he was somebody important. He said, "Now, goddam, this has gone just time enough! Shur'ff says that fair is fair! Now you just come on along."

Austin paused just long enough to give me a wink. Then he was gone down the runway between the cells. I could hear him and Claude. Claude said, "Well, goddam, you lawyers don't seem to mind to take your time!"

And Austin said, "How'd you like to get into a lawsuit for just such talk?"

"I never said nothing! I never did!"

And then they were gone and I was alone in my cell with the prospect of getting out in less than twenty-four hours. Well, I don't know how to tell you how good that felt. The idea of having the Derringer in my hand and Claude right in front of me with them keys looped over his gun butt was damn near more than I could wait for. Talk about a kid waiting for Christmas. Hell, I was worse.

I took me a drink of brandy and then laid down on my bunk and looked at the ceiling. I could say that when black fell that night that I'd be looking at that ceiling for the last time.

And I meant that. Whichever way it went. It mattered to me. Of course I wasn't going to lay there and say that it didn't. For I was a man who valued life. And to say that I was going to give it up without caring would have been a lie. But come the morrow, I was going out of the cell I was in, one way or the other. I was looking at that ceiling for the last time. One way or the other.

I hoped the other would see me free. But I'd had two days of jail time and that was all I wanted.

And all I was going to stand for.

THE TEXAS BANK ROBBING COMPANY

But I had a day and a night to get through before Austin brought me that Derringer the next day and gave me the chance to effect my own release.

Not too long after, Billy yelled down: "That looked like some kind of high-powered lawyer you had there. Kin he do you any good?"

I got up off my cot and went to the cell door. I said, "Billy, the worst old muddlefuddle in the world could do me some good. Because they got the wrong man."

He sang back, "Aw, yeah, brother! Well, if he gets you out, see if he'll work for me. For nothing. Which is what I got to pay."

After a time the sheriff came back, looking a little worried. He said, "Now, say, what is that lawyer of yours going to be up to?"

I said, "Beats the hell out of me. I just pay him, I don't tell him what to do."

The sheriff said, "Well, he's making a lot of noise about you not being able to get a fair trial in Laredo. Now, blame it, that just ain't straight thinkin'. You kin get just as fair a trial here as you will anywhere's else. He says they's too many as knows you here. Well, hell, Wilson, you're known all over the state! Now don't you let him move this here trial! We'll give you as fair a shake as you'll get anywhere."

I tell you, the old fool never ceased to amaze me. You'd of thought it was some children's game we were playing at. I just looked at him, thinking that if I'd of known him before, I'd of concentrated all my outlaw work right there in Laredo. I said, slowly, "Well, I don't know, sheriff. He ain't real happy about the way he was treated. I reckon that was what put the burr under his tail."

The sheriff jerked his head back. "Way he was treated! Why, I told them boys of mine to give him the red carpet!"

I looked down at the floor like I had something I didn't want to admit. I finally said, "Well, it was Claude!"

"Claude! CLAUDE!" He said it loud enough to bring rain.

I kept looking down at the floor. "Yeah," I said. "Claude."

"What in the hell did that addlebrain do!"

I said, "Well, I didn't think it was all that bad. But my lawyer is a little touchy about legal matters. You know them lawyers how they are."

"Well, what the hell did he *do!* Claude."

I shrugged and hesitated like I just hated to tell it. "Well, it had to do with his right to see me in privacy. And you know that's in the Constitution. Anyway, Claude made a big fuss about it. Wanted to stay and listen and all like that. And that was after they'd searched Mr. Austin as clean as a gnat's ass. I don't know what Claude thought he might be trying to smuggle in. Maybe a cannon or a cavalry regiment or a keg of dynamite. Anyway, it made my lawyer a little hot."

The sheriff pursed his mouth and squinted his eyes and kind of nodded as if it was just what he'd been expecting. He said, "So the boy's gone to shur'ffing, has he? Well, we'll see about that! He can't do his own job so he's got to take on mine." He suddenly pushed away from the bars and started up the corridor.

I said, "Now, sheriff—"

But he was gone, going up the corridor saying, "Claude! Claude! CLAUDE, GODDAMMIT!"

I sat there and laughed quietly to myself. I didn't figure that Claude was going to give lawyer Austin much trouble when he came to see me to bring me the Derringer the next morning.

I had a drink and smoked a cigarillo and then Claude came marching up the corridor with two other deputies behind him carrying shotguns. He stopped at my cell door and said, a little coldly, "Mr. Young, if you'll go and stand against that back wall there, I got to search your cell."

I'd been expecting it. As a matter of fact I'd been hoping they would.

After I got up against the wall Claude unlocked the door, taking the loop of keys off the butt of his side gun, and came into the cell. He gave me an apprehensive glance and I said, "Just take it easy, Claude. I ain't going to bite you."

He didn't say a word and I got the strong impression that he was pouting at me. He went around the cell making his inspection. First he went through my bed, lifting up the mattress and looking under it, and then through the blanket. Then he went over and searched the other cot. There wasn't a hell of a lot to search in the sparse cell. He went over to the corner, glanced at the slop bucket, and then lifted the lid of the water keg and looked inside it.

I said, "I got some dynamite in there, Claude. Reckon it'll still go off after sitting in that water?"

But Claude wasn't speaking to me. After he'd finished with the cell he said, "Now, Mr. Young, if you'll just sit down over there on your bunk and take off your boots."

"I'll be glad to."

While I was taking off my boots he stepped to the cell door and handed his pistol to one of the shotgun guards. I had been wondering if he was careless enough to come near me wearing his sidegun. I handed him my boots and he looked inside them and handed them back. "All right, Mr. Young," he said. "You kin put them back on and then stand up. I'm gonna have to search you."

I done as he bid me and, after I'd stood up, he kind of patted me down.

What was curious to me was that I was wearing my hat and he never paid it no mind. I could have had that Derringer perched right up there on top of my head for all he knew. But that wasn't where I was going to hide it next morning, in case they searched again. I already had me a foolproof place picked out.

When he was done Claude give me a kind of hard look and said, "Unnerstan', this wasn't my idea. Shur'ff wanted me to satisfy myself so I'd quit acting like a damn fool. Man tries to do his job and he gets called a damn fool." He gave me an injured look. "But I reckon he had some help in getting me in trouble."

"How's that?"

"You know what I mean."

"I don't either."

"Well, that's all right, Mr. Young. I'll say no more. I ain't one to hold a grudge. But you remember who it's been been seeing to your wants. A fine return I got paid back."

Then he left, locking the cell door and going off

THE TEXAS BANK ROBBING COMPANY

down the corridor as if he'd been done a great wrong. Well, it was working about the way I'd hoped. Billy yelled down and wanted to know what was going on.

"Nothing," I said. "They just been searching my cell. Why don't you reach over there and bang on that door and tell whoever comes that I want to see Claude."

He said, "Seein' Claude is more than I want to do. I ain't even glad to see him when he's bringin' me my vittles."

But I could hear him pounding on the door and then talking to whoever answered. I sat on my bunk and waited on the deputy. He wasn't long in coming. I was pleased to see he came right up to my cell door. I guess since he'd searched me and my cell he was convinced I wasn't holding a deadly weapon.

He said, "What do you be wanting, Mr. Young?"

I said, "Well, Claude, you seem to have a burr under your tail about something. If it's got anything to do with me, I'd like to know."

He said, "You know."

"No I don't."

He kind of reared back a little. "You got me a good ass eatin' from the shur'ff 'bout the way I treated that lawyer feller of yours. You told the shur'ff I was interferin' with him in his natcheral duties."

I shook my head. "No, I didn't. The sheriff wanted to know what had my lawyer so hot under the collar and he asked me some questions and I told him. Couldn't very well do anything else. But I also told him that that was the way lawyers are. They always looking for something to get hot about. I never told the sheriff you done anything."

He said, "Well, I caught me some hell."

I said, "You know I never meant for that to happen. The sheriff is worried that my lawyer may try to move the trial. And—"

"Oh, I know thet!" Claude said. "Goddam, do I know thet! Oh, hell, the shur'ff didn't leave no mistake about thet!"

I said, "So I reckon he just wanted you to understand that my lawyer is going to insist on going by the law."

"God, ain't he!"

"But they ain't no use in me and you having a falling out. Now is there?"

He looked grateful. He said, "Well, naw, Mr. Young, they ain't. An' I appreciate you bein' man enough to have brought this out like you have. You are what I've heerd you was—a gentleman."

I said, trying not to laugh, "I appreciate that, Claude."

He was leaning up against the bars in a comfortable way. "Now, is they anything I can get you? You all fixed up on whiskey and smokes?"

I said, "I'm just fine. In fact I think I'll have a drink right now." I got the opened bottle out from under my bunk, the good brandy Austin had brought me, poured myself a little in a cup, and then walked up and offered Claude the bottle through the bars. He acted like he wanted to flinch back, but he didn't. I said, "Whyn't you have a little snort. Wouldn't hurt. Just one."

He wiped his mouth with the back of his hand and then glanced up the alleyway between the cells. "I ought not to," he said. "But one quick one won't hurt the devil." He took the bottle, took a quick pull, then said, "Why, damn, Mr. Young! That's mighty fine drinkin'."

I said, "Have another."

"Believe I will," he said. And he took another pull, a longer one this time. Then he handed the bottle back through the bars. "I'm much obliged."

"De nada," I said.

I went and sat back down on my bunk. I said, "Are you a family man, Claude?"

"Damn sure am," he said. "Got a missus and two little chirrens."

"Yeah? What's your wife's name?"

"Doris. Girl I growed up with."

"How about your kids? How old are they?"

"Well, the boy's one and the girl is, I believe, goin' on three." He suddenly kind of grinned sheepishly. "I tell you, one of the reasons I never have no breakfast when I come in here to the jail is Doris is nearly worked down by them chirren. She's up all night with them an' ain't able to get up an' fix my breakfast. But I guess I don't mind. But it's been mighty neighborly of you to be hepin' me out like thet."

I said, "I'm just glad to do it, Claude." And I meant it. I could already see it was one of the smartest moves I'd made since they'd throwed me in their hoosegow.

And I reckoned it was going to come home to haunt them.

I settled down to wait. There was nothing else to do. But after an hour of pacing back and forth in my cell I could tell it was going to be one of the longest days and nights I'd ever spent. I chinned myself up on the bars of the windows a few times and looked out, but there wasn't that much to see.

After I ate the noon meal I just lay and smoked and thought. About midafternoon Billy yelled out, "Mr. Young!"

"What?"

"You reckon you'll git out?"

"Why?"

"Aw, I dunno. Man like you. Be a waste him spendin' his time in sech a place."

"How about yourself, Billy?"

That made him cackle. "Me? Hell, I got me three square meals a day an' a dry bed. Thet's 'bout the best one like me kin hope fer. Hell, I'm content. I'm scairt they liable to turn me loose."

I said, "Billy, you can tend to yourself better than anyone else can. Don't sell yourself so short."

"Not at my age, Mr. Young. I'm too old. Tell you the truth, I tried to rob that damn mail coach to git myself throwed in jail."

The balance of that afternoon my mind wandered to what Billy had said. And the thought kept occurring to me that I could end up the same way. But I wouldn't listen to that, I wouldn't have that. I wasn't about to end up staying in a jail just in order to eat.

I'd die first.

Nor was I ever going to be in another jail. This one taste I'd had was all I wanted.

In the late afternoon the sheriff came back. He looked unhappy. He said, "Wilson, they are going to fight me over you. The law in Houston is sendin' down some of their boys to have a talk with you. I reckon you know what that means. They want to take you back there for that Houston job."

I said, "They'll play hell trying. I never done it."

THE TEXAS BANK ROBBING COMPANY

He still looked worried, but he said, "Well, that gladdens my heart to hear you say it. I jest hope you kin make it stick. But they'll be here in two days. Lord hep' us all."

I said, "Don't worry, sheriff."

But he went off shaking his head and looking considerably concerned about the matter.

The night that I thought would never come finally arrived. I did what I'd been doing for what seemed like forever—smoked and drank and lay and stared at the ceiling. I tried not to think about Marianne nor to think about freedom. My only real worry about Marianne was that Austin wouldn't be able to convince her to get on a train and head for San Antonio. But I couldn't go on worrying about that. I had to get some rest, to be ready for what the morrow was going to bring.

I was nervous; nervouser than I'd ever been going in on any job. And I was never a man who could spit right before he walked through the front door of a bank with a drawn pistol. The adventure that was to happen the next day was more important than anything I'd ever done in my life.

I did feel kind of foolish about Austin Davis. And I resolved to myself that, if our plan worked, I'd make it up to him about the way I'd done him. But if nothing else, my capture had shown me that I had true friends and that the woman I loved also loved me and would stick by my side in bad times as well as good.

I finally went to sleep with that thought in my mind.

I awoke the next morning way past my usual getting-up time. One of the deputies was already at the door with a fresh pan of water and soap and a clean towel. I got out of bed slowly. From all the drinking and smoking I'd done the night before my mouth tasted like the underside of a saddle on a lathered-up horse. The deputy was one of the young ones. He left the pan of water sitting in the little window and then stepped back while I took it.

I said, "Thanks."

He just stood there kind of watching me. I went ahead and washed my face and washed my mouth out and then dried off. When I turned around he was still there. I sat down on my cot and lit a cigarillo, coughing a little. I said, "Where's the coffee?"

He said, "I'll git it. Right away."

He left and I sat there, realizing where I was and what was fixing to happen. I tell you, it put a knot in my stomach as big as a cannon ball. All I knew was that in a couple of hours I'd either be free or dead. Wasn't no other way for it. I'd had all the jail I was going to put up with.

When the deputy brought my coffee back, I got it and put a big shot of brandy in with it. I thought the deputy would go then, but he just kept standing there. I said, "Thanks for the coffee."

He said, "Mr. Young, I'm a-gonna ast you a boon."

I looked at him, wondering what the hell kind of favor he thought I could do him. I said, "Yeah?"

"Yessir. They done got a bunch more of them wanted posters in on you. And I was a-wonderin'—I was wonderin', if I was to brang one back and a pencil if you'd write your name on it fer me."

I took the cup away from my mouth and stared at him. "Are you crazy?"

He took it for a serious question. He said, earnestly, "Well, no sir, I don't reckon I am."

I said, "You want an outlaw to sign a poster?"

"Yessir."

"Why?"

He shrugged. "Well, you about the best known man I ever seen."

I just shook my head. "Well, I won't do it. To begin with—what's your name?"

"Tom."

"Well, Tom, to begin with, I ain't Wilson Young. So I can't very well sign his name. And even if I was I ain't sure I'd do it."

"Well, as quick's they prove you is Wilson Young, will you sign it then? Shur'ff says you are."

I didn't know what to say to the boy. I finally just nodded. "All right, Tom. When they prove I'm Wilson Young I'll sign you a poster. But you'll be an old man before that happens."

He said, "Yessir. An' Claude says to tell you he'll be going to get yore breakfast right away. But you's to tell me if you'd be wantin' anythin' different than what you been a-havin'."

I said, "No, eggs and side meat is fine. Just tell him not to forget himself or Billy."

"Yessir. I'll do it."

Now, where the time had passed so slowly it suddenly began to pick up speed like a stream sweeping around a curve in its bed. Claude brought my breakfast and I ate and drank two cups of coffee heavy with brandy. I could feel myself beginning to tense up. Billy hollered down to thank me for the breakfast. He said, "How much longer you plannin' on spendin' this kind of *dinero* on an old worthless like me?"

"Not much longer, Billy," I said. "Not much longer."

Then Claude was coming back to inform me that my lawyer was there.

I took a kind of deep breath. "Send him on back," I said.

"They searchin' him now," he said. "Him and his little carpetbag."

While I waited I wondered what kind of papers Austin was carrying around in his bag and where he got them. Naturally, lawyers always had a bunch of papers in their little grip, but I didn't know where one went to get such a commodity if you weren't a lawyer.

I had another drink and lit a cigarillo and was sitting there smoking and drinking when Claude brought Austin back. Claude was kind of huffy about it. He unlocked the door immediately and said to Austin, "Now I want you to take notice that I never said one word, just opened this cell door right up. Now you kin just go right on in."

Austin said, "Just as it should be, too, by God."

Claude closed and locked the door and then went off up the corridor. Austin sat down, but didn't say anything until we heard the outer door slam. Then he got up and took a look to be sure Claude wasn't shamming.

When he sat back down he said, "What the hell was that all about?"

I told him and he laughed. Then he said, "But maybe that was a pretty good piece of work. They didn't search me near as careful today as they did yesterday."

I said, "They searched the cell yesterday after you left. But I done got that handled."

"Yeah?"

"Yes. I got a place they'll never look for it." Then

I stopped and looked at him. "You have got it with you."

He nodded. "Oh, yes. Let me glance down the hall and then I'll hand it to you."

I said, "You got a handkerchief?"

"Sure."

"Give it to me."

He took a white handkerchief out of the inside pocket of his coat and handed it to me. I said, "Take a quick look and then hand me the gun."

He stepped to the bars, glanced toward the office door, and then came back to the cot. With his back to the cell door he unbuckled his belt, exposed the back of the buckle, tripped some little catch, and a back plate came off. Inside I could see the Derringer. He pulled some little clips loose that were holding it and swiftly handed it to me. It took me but a second to wrap it in the handkerchief. Then I stepped across the cell and dropped it in the slop bucket.

Behind me I heard Austin laugh softly. He said, "That's going to be a little messy."

I said grimly, "I'd swim through a mile of shit to get out of here."

"You sure it won't get too damp?"

I shook my head. "Naw, I can dry it off. It takes a good long while for cartridges to be bothered by water."

He got his belt rebuckled and then sat back down on the cot, opening his little bag to make it look like we were talking lawyer business in case anyone came along. He said, "Well, it looks like we are getting about ready to do it. How you feel?"

"Nervous," I said. "I'd hate to have to spit. On a bet."

He said, "How you got it figured?"

I said, "Yesterday they come and searched the cell about thirty minutes after you were here. I reckon they'll do the same today. About a quarter of an hour after that I'm going to call Claude back. I expect he'll come along like he did yesterday. If he don't I'll just keep calling him back until he comes by himself. After that I'll throw down on him, get out of this cell, get in that office, and crack the door for ya'll to come in."

He nodded. "That's the way to do it. Right after I leave here, me and Chulo and Wilcey will take up a position right across the street."

"Not in a bunch," I said.

"Oh, hell no, Will. We ain't that dumb. Won't nobody notice us."

"You know you got to watch Chulo."

He said, "Listen, I done got that mean Meskin straightened out. I don't know why, but he's scairt to death of you. He'll do exactly what I tell him. But when you crack that door I'm coming straight in. Chulo will come and stand right beside the jail house door. Then if anyone wants to come in he'll escort them through the door with a gun in their back. Wilcey will be across the street with the horses, yours will be there of course. Then after that we put the sonofabitches in the cells and just waltz out of here as pretty as you please."

I said, "All right, that sounds fine. Now what about Marianne?"

He said, "She ought to be getting on a train in about an hour, headed for San Antonio. She'll be waiting for you there."

184

I kind of cocked my head at him. "Just that easy? She agreed that easy?"

He looked kind of uncertain. He said, "Yeah, she said that was just fine with her."

I sat there and looked at him a long half a moment. I said, "I don't believe that, Austin. She's packed and ready to go? On the morning train?"

He put his hand to his face. "No, she ain't. She wouldn't go. I told her what you said, told her everything you said, but it didn't do one goddam bit of good. Will, I tell you, that woman's got a mind of her own and wasn't nothing I could do about it. I told her I'd lie one time for her, but that was all. Now I've lied when I told you she was taking the morning train."

"When is she going?"

"She won't leave town until she sees you out of jail. There's an afternoon train and she says she'll be on that one if you get free."

"Goddammit!" I said. "Goddam that damn woman! You go right back there and get her on the morning train. You tell her once I break jail they will be coming to look for her! Hasn't she got a lick of sense? You tell her if she ain't on that morning train I am going to blister her ass red! And I mean it!"

Boy, I was hot, and no mistake. Here I was about to embark on as dangerous an undertaking as I'd ever tried and the goddam woman didn't have sense enough to get out of the way.

Austin said, "All right. I'll tell her, but I ain't sure she'll listen."

"You are going to have to make her listen! Get it through her goddam hard head that she'll be the first one they'll come looking for when I'm free of this place.

And the first thing they'll do is slap a pair of wrist manacles on her and lead her down to this jail with hopes of luring me back! You tell her she is endangering me! You tell her to get her ass on that train!"

"I'll do it, Will. Now you take it easy."

"No, I won't take it easy! You let a goddam woman become your running mate and they get to thinking they are as smart as you. You tell her she is damn brand new to this outlaw game and she is to follow my lead until she gets sense enough to pour piss out of a boot with the directions on the heel! Now you tell her to get on that train! She is worrying me! For once in her goddam stiff-necked life she is to follow orders!"

He said, "Then I better hurry."

I said, "You damn well better."

He got up and stuck his hand out kind of awkwardly. He said, "I'll see you on the outside."

I stood up and took his hand. "Austin, want you to know how much I appreciate this. If I get out of here alive, I ain't going to let this go unnoticed. You will be my partner as long as you want to be."

Be goddam if he didn't kind of pat me on the shoulder. "You'll get out alive. They ain't going to hold Wilson Young. We'll be waiting to see that door crack."

"Thanks."

Then he turned and went to yelling for Claude. The door opened immediately, almost as if the deputy had been a-waiting the summons. When Claude got there and unlocked the door, Austin turned to me and said, formally, "Mr. Wilson, I want you to know that I'll be doing everything possible to right this wrong. They are holding an innocent man."

THE TEXAS BANK ROBBING COMPANY

"Thank you, Mr. Davis," I said. "I appreciate all your efforts."

Then we shook hands formally and Austin went out the door. As they walked up the corridor I heard Claude say, "Well, I hope you are satisfied this time. And ain't going to be causin' me no more trouble with the shur'ff."

I heard Austin say, "Just doing my job. That's all. No hard feelings."

After I heard the door shut I sat down to wait. Billy sang out, "I never heerd of a man could afford a lawyer comin' to see him two days runnin'. Lord, the money you do spend!"

I didn't answer him back, just kind of mumbled to myself, "Lord, I hope it don't all come to aught."

They came, just as I'd guessed, within a half an hour. I was glad they were that predictable. And they did the same thing they'd done the day before. I stiffened up when Claude went near the slop bucket, but he only wrinkled his nose and said, "Somebody ought to empty that thing pretty soon."

Of course that sent a chill through me. But they weren't likely to, not in time, not before I made my break.

Then, after they'd searched me, Claude lingered a moment outside my cell door. He said, "You know, Mr. Young, you are a mighty fine gentleman. I went home last night and told Doris about you havin' ast after her and the chirren. Course she's all excited about you bein' here. It's in all the papers an' all the neighbors keep comin' over to ast her about you. Makes her feel like a real queen."

I said, "I'm mighty glad to hear that, Claude. Any

little thing I can do. What did you say the names of your two children were?"

He beamed just a little. "Well, it's Mary. That's the girl. And little Claude. I'm mighty proud of that boy."

"I bet you are," I said. "I bet you are."

Then he was gone and the time was very near. I poured myself out a good stiff drink, downed that, and then had another. After that I went over and fished around in the slop bucket until I came out with the handkerchief-wrapped Derringer. It was disgusting work, but it had to be done.

I took it back to my cot, unwrapped the handkerchief, flung it on the floor, and then very carefully began cleaning off the gun, paying especial attention to the primer end of the cartridges and the firing pin. When I had done that I looked at the Derringer for a moment, cradling it in the palm of my hand, thinking of it as my ticket out of that goddam jail. Then I stuck it down in the rear of my waistband. After that I walked up to the cell door and yelled down for Billy to hammer on the door and call Claude.

"Do I tell him anythin'?"

"No, just call him back here."

He pounded and I heard the door open and someone come in. But it wasn't Claude, it was one of the other deputies. He said, "Claude has just stepped down the street for a minute. What can I hep' you with?"

"Nothing," I said. "Nothing. Just tell him to get in here as quick's he gets back."

I needed Claude and the ring of keys he looped over his gun butt so carelessly.

Well, I waited; I waited and I worried. I don't know how long the time was, maybe a half hour maybe more.

And all the time I was worrying about how it was going to mess up the timing for Wilcey and Austin and Chulo. I didn't know how soon they'd get in position across the street or how long they could wait.

So I just sat there and drank brandy and smoked cigarillos and worried.

No, I didn't really worry. I'd made up my mind that it didn't matter if something went wrong. I wasn't staying in that jail anymore. I had a loaded gun, never mind it only had two bullets in it; I had a loaded gun and I was going out of that jail before noon one way or the other.

Marianne had left my mind, my partners had left my mind. All had left my mind except my need to be free. I could not be caged. I could not be held behind bars. The spirit within me would die and I would just as soon be dead in the body that God had given me as to be trapped by steel walls and the will of other men.

I poured myself out another drink of brandy and sat there facing the cell door. I sat that way for only a few minutes and then I got up and walked to the cell window. I pulled myself up and looked outside; there were free people out there and I would be joining them very quickly. They weren't going to hold me. They might hold my corpse, but that's all they would have.

I knew that I had made up my mind. I knew that when Claude came back and I told him I'd kill him he'd believe me, for I knew that I meant it. And that's the surest way in the world to bluff in a poker game. You might be holding only a pair of deuces, but you bet them like they are four aces. And when you look down at that pair of deuces, you don't see a lowly pair, you see four aces. When you do that the man across the table will believe you.

Then I heard the corridor door open and shut. I turned toward the front of my cell. I could feel the weight of the Derringer in the back of my waistband.

It was Claude. He came up looking kind of hot and bothered. I didn't look at his face; I looked at his hip.

The loop of keys was hung over his gun butt as always. I said, "Claude, I had something I wanted to talk to you about."

He said, "Mr. Young, I'd appreciate it if you'd just make it kind of quick. We got some trouble outside of town and the shur'ff wants me to head out that way."

I got off my bunk and started toward the cell door. He fell back, backing up until his back was against the bars of the opposite cell. He said, "Mr. Young, now what was it?"

I said, "It's this, Claude." I took the Derringer out of my waistband and stuck my hand through the bars and pointed it straight at his heart. It was about two feet from his chest. I said, "Claude, don't move and don't make a sound or I will kill you. This is a .38 caliber Derringer and it's got two cartridges in it. If you do anything, I'll kill you."

His face went slack. He said, "Oh, no, Mr. Young! Oh, no!"

Chapter Eight

I said, "Get your hands above your head, Claude! Now! Do it!"

After a second he slowly raised his hands shoulder high. He said, "Mr. Young, where did you get that thing? Oh, hell! The shur'ff is goin' to kill me!"

I said, "Claude, don't you make a sound. I want you to do exactly as I tell you or I will shoot you straight through the heart. If you value your life, you better believe me."

He just stared at me, still too shocked to know what was happening. He said, "This is a dirty trick, Mr. Young. We treated you right! We let yore wife come see you, we brung you whiskey and smokes, we let you order yore food out. How come you to do this?"

I said, "Now, Claude, I want you to do exactly as I tell you. If you don't do it just right I will shoot you. I want you to take your keys off your gun butt and step over here and unlock the door. Then I want you to step back to right where you are. Now do it right now."

He said, "Mr. Young, I can't do that. The shur'ff would have my hide."

"Claude, you don't get it. The sheriff can't have your hide if you are dead. Now do what I tell you."

He kind of half smiled. "Mr. Young, you wouldn't shoot me. You are too nice a feller."

I pointed my arm a little straighter toward his chest and tightened my grip around the Derringer. I said, "Claude, I'm running out of time. This Derringer is cocked and my finger is on the trigger. There are two bullets in it. I will kill you with the first one. Chances are you will hit that cell wall behind you and fall forward. Then I'll get the keys. They'll hear the shot, but I'll kill the first man through the door with the second cartridge in this gun. After that they will wait and talk. By then I will have those keys and I'll be out of this cell and have your pistol and all the cartridges that you got in your belt. Before they take me I will have killed a dozen men." I was watching his face as he listened to me. I said, "Yes, Claude, I'll kill you. And then it won't matter about the sheriff taking the hide off you."

I could see him beginning to understand what was happening. He said, "Now don't you be hasty, Mr. Young."

I said, "Claude, you better think about your wife Doris and your little girl Mary and little Claude. I'm going to give you five seconds and then they are going to be without a father."

He stared at me, his hands still at his shoulders.

I said, "One, two three—"

He said, "I'm a-coming! Just don't git hasty!"

I pulled my arm back as he started for the cell door. He took the ring of keys off his gun butt, found the right one, and unlocked my cell door. I said, "Now get back over there! Back up! And turn your face to the wall! Do it!"

He done as I told him and I took my left hand, still watching him, and slowly pushed the cell door open.

I was, by God, free out of the cage they'd put me in!

I stepped through the door and took his pistol out of its holster, transferring the Derringer to my trouser waistband.

Then I stood there for just a second, a revolver, a heavy Colt revolver in my hand once again, and kind of breathed deeply.

I reached out and took Claude by the collar of his shirt and said, "Now, Claude, I want you to turn to your left. We are going to walk down and you are going to open that door and we are going to go out into that office." I nudged him in the back of the head with the barrel of his revolver. "And, Claude, this here is your own gun. I've already seen that it is loaded." I pulled the hammer back with my thumb. It went *clitch-clatch*. I said, "You probably know better than I do what kind of hair trigger it's got on it."

His voice kind of shook. He said, "Mr. Young, please be careful! That sonofabitch will go off if you breath on it! Shur'ff done warned me about it!"

I said, "It's up to you, Claude, whether it goes off or not. Now you turn to your left."

He turned, slowly, like he was walking on eggs, and then we started up the corridor, me right behind him with my left hand holding the collar of his shirt and my right hand holding the revolver that was pointed dead at the back of his head.

I said, "Claude, if you take a sneezing fit it will be the death of you. By that I mean you had better not flinch one inch. Do you understand me?"

"Yessir. Yessir, Mr. Young, I understand you." And then the damn fool said, "But Mr. Young, I want you to know I'm mighty disappointed in you, you doin' me this away. After the good turns I done you."

I said, "Claude, did you want me to rot in that cell? Did you think I wanted to go to prison? Which is where I was headed!"

He said, "Well, no sir. I never thought of that."

And then we were passing Billy's cell. He was almost jumping up and down, slapping his knee in silent glee. "Oh, Mr. Young," he said, "I knowed you'd do it! Oh by damn, oh by damn!"

I said, "Billy, now you hold it down."

He said, "Oh, yessir. I heerd every goddam word of it! Goddam, if you ain't the beatenist!" And he slapped his knee again. "You are the cat's pajamas and no mistake!"

I said, "Billy, now you just wait until I get this tended to and then I'll unlock your cell."

He said, "Oh, by God! Oh, by God! I'd jest as lief git out of here just to tell about it! Wilson Young! I'll be damned!"

I said to him, "Billy, take it easy. Let me tend to this."

We were at the door. I said to Claude, "Now, Claude, you open that door. Do it very carefully. No, wait a minute. I want some of your cartridges."

He had a belt full of them and I took about six or

seven out and shoved them in my pocket, letting go of his collar, but keeping the gun barrel right against the back of his head. A man never knows when he might need more cartridges.

Then I said, "Now you open that door. And you do it carefully. You are going to pull it all the way back and then me and you is going through it. Now you tell me right now before we do that who is in that office."

He said, "I don't rightly know."

I punched him in the back of the head with the barrel of his pistol. I said, "You goddam well better know. Your life may depend on it."

He said, "Well, they was two deputies in there when I come back. That young one, Tom, and another'n. But I don't rightly know if they still there."

I poked him with the gun. "You better be sure, Claude! Unless you want the back of your brains going through your eyes."

A little note of scared came into his voice. He said, "Now, Mr. Young! I can't be sure who's in there."

I said, "What about the sheriff. Is he there?"

"Not when I left. No sir, he wasn't. But he might have come back. I just don't want to be held accountable."

Through my arm on his back, the one that was holding his collar, I could feel him beginning to tremble. I wanted him scared; I wanted him to know that I'd kill him if he made a false move. I said, "All right, reach out and get that door handle and open it wide. Then me and you is going right through. You better rein off this hand of mine on your collar like a good horse. You just go the way you get pointed. You understand?"

"Yessir," he said.

"All right. Open that door."

He reached out and got the knob and pulled it back. I pulled him toward me a little so it would clear. Then he and I stepped through. There were three of the deputies in the office. One was sitting at the sheriff's desk with his feet up; another was at the other desk, working on some papers; the third was leaning against the wall staring out the front window. They didn't even glance our way when we came in. And if they had, I doubt they'd of seen me behind Claude, so big and wide was he. Other than their side guns they weren't armed.

I said, "Freeze! Now!"

They glanced up, the two at the desks turning their heads to see who was making all the commotion. I had backed up against the wall so that I had all three of them in front of me. I said, "I'm Wilson Young and you had better move. I can kill all three of you before you can bat an eye!"

The one looking out the front window was the young one. He just stood there staring, his mouth open. I said, "You two at the desks! Get up by that front wall. And keep your hands away from your guns or you are dead! Now move, dammit! Move!"

One of them found his voice. He said, "What is this, Claude?"

There was a little quiver in Claude's voice. He said, "I reckon you ought to do like he says. I reckon he means it."

"Move!" I told them again. "Get up there and line up against that wall. I'm going to shoot you in the next two seconds if you don't!"

That got their attention. They got up and quickly

walked to the front wall and stood by the deputy that was already there. Of course they didn't have much choice. I was so well hidden behind Claude that they couldn't have gotten a shot off at me unless they wanted to shoot at Claude and, by then, I'd of killed all three.

They stood there staring at me behind Claude, not so much scared as just kind of startled at the sudden turn of events. I said, "Now take off your gun belts. Do it very carefully. Just let them drop at your feet. I don't want to hurt none of you boys, but if you make me do it, I will."

They all got their gun belts unbuckled and let them drop at their feet. Then I nodded at the one nearest the door. "You there—Just reach your right hand over and crack that door. Just pull it back about six inches. No more. And don't get no idea about jumping through it. I'd kill you before you took half a step."

He done as he was told, turning the knob and just pulling the door back enough so that Austin would be able to see it. "All right," I said. "Now you three get over toward that side of the wall and lay flat on your faces. Just spread eagle yourselves out on the floor." I waved the pistol to show them which direction I wanted them to move. When they had done that I shoved Claude away from me. "Now, Claude, you get over there and join your friends. Just walk over there and get on your face. And don't look back."

When I had them all safely on the floor I turned to face the door. After a moment it was pushed back slightly. A voice said, lowly, "Will?"

"Yes," I said.

Austin Davis came quickly through the door and shut it behind him. He said, "Chulo's right outside."

Then he looked at the deputies on the floor. "Looks like you got things in hand in here."

"Yeah," I said. "Let's get them back into a cell. You cover them for there's something I want to do first." I walked over by the chief deputy. "Claude, where's my revolver and gun belt?"

He had his face pressed down against the floor so that his voice came out muffled. "In the drawer in the shur'ff's desk."

While Austin held a gun on them I found my revolver and gun belt in the right hand top drawer of the desk. After I strapped it on, I realized how naked I'd felt without it. I shoved Claude's gun down in my belt and drew my own, familiar piece. I checked and it was loaded. Then I said, "All right, let's put them in a cell."

Austin snapped out, "All right, you sonofabitches! Get on your feet!"

I said, "Now partner, ain't no call to talk to them like that. They were pretty nice to me during my little stay here."

Austin grinned. I'd never seen his face get hard before. It kind of impressed me. He said, "All right, you heard the man. So you *nice* sonofabitches get on your feet."

I said, "That's better."

They got up. As soon as they turned, Claude looked at Austin with astonishment. Then he glanced at me. He said, "Mr. Young, this here is yore lawyer! He ain't supposed to be engagin' in this sort of monkey business!"

I said, "He specializes in getting people out of jail.

THE TEXAS BANK ROBBING COMPANY

One way or the other. Now ya'll walk back toward the cells. Do it real careful. And keep your hands up."

Just as they were about to go through the door I noticed a wanted poster of me tacked to the wall. I said to Austin, "Cover them for a second." Then I jerked the poster off the wall and took it to the desk. There were several pencils there and I took one and wrote across the front: "To the gentlemen of the Webb County jail. Thanks for your hospitality . . . Wilson Young."

Austin was looking at me and grinning. "Always leave your calling card," he said. "When you want to be welcome back."

I said, "Not likely." Then I got behind my four captives. I said, "All right, now just march on through the door and to the very back. I'm going to let you boys have my old cell."

As we passed Billy's cage he was jumping up and down and slapping his knee and chortling. Claude growled, "Aw, shut up, Billy!"

Billy said, "Goddammit, Mr. Young, give 'em a taste of they own medicine! See how they like it! Whoooooh hah!"

I said, "Billy, just hold it down. I'll be right back to unlock your cell."

I herded my deputies to my cell. The door was still open with the loop of keys still hanging in the lock. I said, "Inside, boys." They crowded in, lowering their hands as they went through the door. I slammed the door after the last one was in and turned the key. Claude said, "Mr. Young, will you tell me how you come to get that little Derringer?"

I said, "I had it in my boot, Claude. The whole time."

He gaped at me. "I looked in yore boot, Mr. Young. And there weren't no Derringer in there."

"Guess you missed it." I dropped the wanted poster through the bars. "Here, Tom," I said. "Here's the little souvenir you wanted."

He said, "I'm much obliged, Mr. Young."

But Claude said, "Lord, Mr. Young, we are in plenty of hot water. When the shur'ff gets back and see what—"

About that time I heard Austin say something from the front office. I turned quickly. Then I heard another voice, loud, say: "Oh, goddammit! No. No. NO!"

Then in another few seconds the sheriff was coming through the corridor door with his hands in the air. Right behind him was Austin, grinning. He said, "Got another customer for you."

I opened the cell door. The sheriff passed me without a word, his head down. But once he was inside the cell, he said, "Wilson, you know this will be the ruin of me. I won't be able to get elected dog catcher now."

I locked the door. "I hate that, sheriff. But just like you had your job, I had mine. No hard feelings." I gave them a little wave. "We'll be leaving now and I don't reckon we'll be staying around town. Tell them boys that turned me in for the reward that they'll have to get out and get an honest job. By the way, sheriff, if I had time I'd like to stay here and press charges against them for attempted road agentry. That was no lie when I told you they tried to hold me and my partners up on the road into town. Maybe you could arrest them before they go to giving people trouble."

He said, "Well, there's no hard feelings, Wilson. But

THE TEXAS BANK ROBBING COMPANY

I damn sure would like to know how you got a gun into your cell. I know that damn supposed lawyer of you'n didn't have it 'cause we searched him from the skin out. That was a pretty good dodge. Fooled the hell out of me. Hell, I thought sure he was a high-powered lawyer."

I said, "Sheriff, the gun was in my boot. One of my boot's got a hollow heel."

He said, "I'll be damned!"

I give them a little wave. "Don't be in no rush to get out."

Then I turned and went down the corridor, trying to figure out which key unlocked Billy's cell. But he was standing up by the door, holding onto the bars. He said, "Mr. Young, ain't no use unlockin' my cell. I ain't got no place to go. I'd just as lief stay in here."

I said, "Goddam, Billy, you don't want to stay in that cell. You can't go with us, but at least you'll be on the loose."

He shook his head. "Thank'ye much, but I ain't got nowheres to go. At least in here I get to eat and got a blanket fer myself."

From the door Austin said, "Will, we better get a move on. We've wasted a pretty good bit of time."

I said, "Yeah, I know." I looked at Billy a moment more trying to think of something to say to him, something that would make him see that freedom was more important than food or a roof over his head. But all I saw was a tired old man who needed to stay in out of the cold when the winter came.

I said, "You sure, Billy?"

He nodded. "Yeah, but I'm much obliged fer the thinking of me."

I said to Austin, "You got any money on you?"

"Sure," he said.

"Give me twenty dollars."

He went into his pocket and came out with two ten-dollar bills. I took them from his hand and handed them through to Billy. "Here, make them let you buy some whiskey from time to time. It'll take the chill out of the night air."

Austin said, "Will, we got to go. Now."

I said, *"Adiós,* Billy. *Buena suerte."* Good luck.

He said, "Take'r slow, Mr. Young. Tell 'em where you got it an' how easy it was."

We went out the office door, me closing it behind us. Then I went to the sheriff's desk and started looking through drawers. Austin said, "What the hell you doing now?"

"Looking for any other rings of keys. You look in that other desk. If they ain't no keys, it will slow them down a little more."

"Right." He went to the desk the deputies used and done like I was doing. In a moment he said, "Here's a bunch."

"Bring them with you."

We started for the door, but I suddenly put out a hand and stopped Austin. I said, "What about Marianne? Did she get on that train?"

He said, "Yeah, I don't believe it, but she did. I had to talk long and hard. But when I told her what you said, that she was endangering you by staying, she seen the light. She's heading for San Antonio and she'll be wherever it is that ya'll stay there."

"All right. Let's get out of here." I shoved the key

THE TEXAS BANK ROBBING COMPANY

ring inside my shirt and Austin did likewise. We stepped through the door and into the sunshine of the outside.

Well, it was a moment like none I'd ever had before. After the confinement, after the long ago moment when they'd put their steel manacles on my wrist, after their bars and the slop buckets and the having to be at their mercy for whiskey and cigarillos and food. I was a free man again; I was my own man again.

Chulo was standing right by the door, lounging up against the wall of the jail. He grinned, his teeth white in his big, black, mean-looking face. He said, *"Como está, mi amigo."*

I said, "Pretty damn good, you mean Meskin. Let's get gone."

We crossed the street to where Wilcey was sitting his horse. The other three were tied to the little iron rings in the concrete sidewalk they had there for that purpose. I was damn glad to see my horse again. I put my foot in the stirrup and swung up in the saddle. It felt damn good to have a fast horse between my legs again. Wilcey, who was just to my right, reached out and touched me kind of awkwardly on the shoulder. He said, "Well, have you had enough of a vacation?"

He was having a hard time keeping the smile off his face.

I said, "Yes. And thanks, partner."

He put out his hand and we shook briefly. We was both kind of embarrassed.

There were people passing up and down the sidewalk, but other than giving us a curious glance, they weren't paying any attention.

Austin said, "We better get."

I said, "Now we just take it slow. We don't attract any attention."

I was about to turn my horse out into the street, when I suddenly thought of something. I said, "Goddammit, I forgot my money. They got four hundred dollars of mine."

Austin said, "Forget it, Will!"

I said, "Hell, no, they done stole three days out of my life. They ain't fixing to steal my goddam money, too."

Wilcey said, "Now cm'on, Will! We got to get out of here. You ain't got time to go back in that jail."

Austin said, "Likely it's in the safe and the safe's going to be locked. You'd have to get the sheriff out of his cell and make him open it and that would take hell's own kind of time. Let's go, Will. Marianne is waiting for you."

I don't know, for some reason it made me just angry as hell. They'd taken me and thrown me in jail, handcuffed me, confined me, insulted me, treated me like a misfit. And now they'd kept my money. I was just hot as hell about the matter. But Austin and Wilcey were right; we didn't have time to go back in the jail. It would have been a fool's play.

"All right," I said. I turned my horse's head out into the street.

Austin said, "Which way we heading?"

I said, "We're heading out just like we are aiming for Mexico. Except we ain't going over the International Bridge. We'll just walk our horses on up the street like we are the most law-abiding citizens in town."

We done it, riding two and two so as not to crowd any of the traffic that was meeting us.

THE TEXAS BANK ROBBING COMPANY

So far nobody had paid us no more mind than if we were out for a Sunday ride.

I was in front, riding on the side toward the buildings. I was still angry as hell, a strange thing, perhaps, for a man who was just out of jail, but then I'd never felt I'd of ought to have been in jail in the first place. Or if I did deserve to be in jail, I thought there was an awful lot of folks like politicians and carpetbaggers and scalawags that should have been there first.

We had ridden perhaps two blocks, just easing our way out of town, when I suddenly stopped my horse. Right to my left was the Laredo National Bank. They had it painted on the front over the door. Wilcey said, "Now what?"

I pointed. I said, "I'm going to rob that goddam bank."

There wasn't a word said for a minute and then Wilcey said, "Have you lost your mind? We are trying to break you out of jail, not rob no damned bank."

I said, "This town robbed me. I'm behind right now. And I ain't never done a goddam thing to Laredo. So I'll be damned if I'll leave here the loser. I am going to rob that bank."

Austin said, "Now, Will, I know you feel strong about this, but—" And then he couldn't help himself, he started laughing. He said, "Boy, wouldn't that be something! Break jail and rob a bank at the same time!"

I said, "I'm going to do it!"

But Wilcey started looking nervous. He was riding just to my right and he sat there, sitting his horse, and said, "Will, we can't do this! That sheriff and his deputies are probably screaming their heads off right now!

It won't be five minutes before they are out and looking for us."

I got off my horse and handed him the reins. "It won't take me two minutes to rob that bank. I ain't leaving here with this town owing me and that's a fact! So you just shut up, gramma!" I looked at the bank. It was just a little affair, not even any plate-glass windows in the front. And just the one door leading in from the street.

Wilcey said, "Now, Will, you ain't planned this job out just right! You never do a job you ain't planned!"

I said, "Shut up, Wilcey. I got all the goddam law in town locked up in their own jail. Couldn't be a better time."

"You're crazy! You're crazy."

I said, "Chulo, you come with me. Austin, you and Wilcey sit out here and hold the horses. We won't be a minute. I ain't going for the vault, just what money they got in the teller cages. We ought to be back out in two minutes. I just want to show a profit."

Austin was laughing, but Wilcey was about to have kittens. He said, "Goddam, if this ain't the craziest thing you ever done, it's damn close to it! I ain't sure I'm gonna stick around for this foolishness!"

I said, "Aw, shut up, old woman. Just sit here and tend to your knitting!"

Chulo had got off his horse. He was giving me that goddam big-toothed grin of his. He said, "We rob one bank?"

I said, "Damn right." Then I told him, "Now, look, we are going to walk in there with drawn pistols and stick up the teller cages. You just make sure don't nobody get cute. I'll see to the money."

I was untying my saddlebags so as to have something to hold the cash we were going to rob them of. I said to Chulo, "But don't you shoot nobody unless you just have to." I looped the saddlebag over my arm, loosened my revolver in its holster, and said, "We'll be right back."

Then we started for the door of that bank.

Chapter Nine

We stopped in front of the bank door. I looked over at Chulo. "You ready, Meskin?"

"*Sí,*" he said. "They have our moneys."

"Yeah, our moneys." I loosened my revolver one more time. Then I opened the door and stepped through. Chulo was right behind me. As soon as he'd shut the door I drew my pistol and said, "This is a robbery!"

It was a pretty small bank, kind of rectangular shaped. Just to the left were three tellers' cages with some desks behind them. There weren't but a couple of customers in the place, and maybe three or four employees behind the cages. There was a little railing to the left of the cages, with a little swinging door so people could go in and out. When I said what I'd said about it being a robbery everyone looked my way and just kind of froze.

I said, in a loud voice: "I'M WILSON YOUNG!

THE TEXAS BANK ROBBING COMPANY

AND I'M GOING TO ROB THIS BANK! DO WHAT I TELL YOU OR YOU WILL BE SHOT!"

They just stared at me with their mouths open. There was about an equal mixture of men and women in the place. I said, "Chulo, keep your gun on them and shoot the first sonofabitch that looks crosseyed!"

I had my saddlebag over my left arm and my drawn revolver in my right hand. I went through the little swinging door, going behind the tellers' cages. There were two men and two women back there. I waved my gun at them. "Get the hell away from the money drawers. And get on the floor. Get facedown on the floor! NOW!"

Well, they fell back from the tellers' counter like they'd been blowed by a high wind. I pointed to the floor with my gun. "Get on your faces! Move it!"

They were getting down, the women having an awkward time, when the door to a little back office opened and a man came out. He was one of them portly, well-dressed banker-looking fellers. He was smoking a cigar. He said, "What in the name of heaven is going—"

And then he saw me. I guess he was the president of the place. But that didn't make no never mind to me. I said, "Get on the floor, mister! Or I'll blow your head off. And I ain't in a very good mood right now!"

He had his cigar clamped in his jaw, and when his mouth went slack, the cigar fell to the floor. I said, "You better follow it! On your face! MOVE, GOD-DAMMIT!"

When he hit the floor I had them all spread-eagled. I stepped over one lady who seemed to be kind of crying. I said, "Excuse me. But I got to get up here to where the money is."

I got to the counter and I just went down the line, jerking open those teller drawers and shoving the money into my saddlebags. I had no idea how much I was getting. In one drawer there was a pretty good pile of hundred-dollar bills. I didn't bother with the small stuff; just took the fifties and twenties and the hundreds and shoved them in the pouches of my saddlebags. They had some gold coins and I grabbed up some of them, but I left the silver as being too heavy.

I hit all three of them teller drawers in less time than it takes to tell. Then I was backing out the little swinging door with a bagful of money over my arm. I said, "Don't forget, I'm Wilson Young. And I don't like Laredo!"

I whirled and motioned at Chulo. He had the two customers facedown on the floor. I said, "Let's git, Chumacho!"

He come, backing up, toward the front of the bank. But then, just as we got to the door, it opened and two men came in. They were about ordinary-looking citizens, ranchers or something, except both of them were wearing a pistol at their sides. I couldn't imagine, for the life of me, how Wilcey and Austin had just let them come on in. For a second we stared at each other. And then one of the women, from behind the tellers' cages, screamed out: "Help, we are being robbed!"

The first one stared at me for an instant, and then his eyes dropped to the gun in my hand. I didn't pause, just slung my revolver in a short, chopping arc and hit him up beside the head. He keeled over without a word. The one behind him was making grabbing motions at the pistol at his side. I stepped forward and kicked him in the belly. He groaned and fell forward and I took a swing at him with the pistol in my hand, but he was falling too fast and I missed. I said to Chulo, "Let's get out of here!"

We ran through the door and out into the street. Wilcey was on foot, trying to hold my horse and Chulo's horse. Austin was still mounted, the reins to Wilcey's horse in his hands.

I yelled, "Goddammit! What's going on out here! Get mounted, get mounted!"

My horse was jumping around, though not as bad as the way Chulo's was. I stood beside my mount, hurriedly tying on the saddlebags with the money in them. Wilcey had turned Chulo's reins over to him and was trying to get mounted himself. But his horse was jumping around so much he was having trouble getting in the saddle. I yelled at Austin, "What the hell happened out here! What's going on?"

Austin said, "A bee stung Chulo's horse and he went to bucking and Wilcey had to get down to hold him."

I said, "Goddammit! Can't ya'll do anything!"

I finished tying on the saddlebags, stuck my foot in the stirrup, and vaulted aboard my horse. Chulo had mounted. Only Wilcey was still having trouble. "Get aboard, get aboard!" I yelled at him.

I rode out into the middle of the street and wheeled my horse to face back toward the bank. Passersby on the street had stopped and were staring at us. I was wielding my pistol in their direction and most of them were shrinking back. Then Wilcey got mounted. But almost in that same instant, the door of the bank opened and the man that I'd kicked in the stomach suddenly came through, his revolver in his hand, and dropped to one knee and began firing at us. My horse was plunging and rearing. I fired at him as best I could. I could hear the bullets singing overhead and whistling past my ear. Someone else, from a little way up the street, was also firing. I emptied about three chambers of my revolver at the man in the door of the bank. I couldn't see where else the firing was coming from. I didn't hit the man, for it was difficult shooting off my horse who had begun to plunge and rear. But the man jumped back inside.

I put spurs to my horse and headed up the street. I was yelling, "Git! Git! Git! Let's git!"

My partners were riding with me, spurring their horses and leaning low over the necks of their mounts just as I was doing. We swept down the street, being stared at by the onlookers on the sidewalk. The street we were on led straight to the International Bridge and Mexico. But I had no intention of going that route. There was a little road that was called the river road that turned off just short of the bridge. That was my goal as we went pounding up the main street of Laredo, trying to get out of town. Behind us the gunfire was still exploding, but we'd desisted trying to answer it. It was more important, now, to ride as fast as we could.

I was on the inside of the street with Wilcey to my right and just a little behind. Austin was on the outside and slightly ahead. Chulo was between Austin and Wilcey.

We raced up the few blocks of the dusty street toward the bridge and then there was the little river road, a road that ran right alongside the American edge of the Rio Grande. I took us sweeping around that. The gunfire was no longer behind us and no more bullets were singing around our ears.

Austin yelled, "Where we headed?"

"To Mexico!" I yelled back. "There's a crossing about a mile ahead!"

I pulled my horse down to a gallop. We'd been running them pretty hard. I wasn't worried about any kind of organized pursuit. Hell, we had all the law in town locked up in their own jail cells.

I yelled, "We are going to lope along here until I spot the low water crossing I know. After that we'll cross into Mexico."

I had it all thought out. That last night in my jail cell, laying on that goddam cot, I'd had nothing better to do.

Well, they hadn't held Wilson Young. They'd thought they were going to, but with the help of my friends and partners, I'd sprung free.

And no one was ever again going to hold me against my will. Marianne was the only person who'd put bonds on me and she'd only do that because I was willing.

Then I heard Chulo yelling at me. He was saying, "Weelson! Weelson! Look back!"

I turned in my saddle. Only to hear Austin saying, "Will, Wilcey is shot! He's bleeding!"

I hadn't realized how far he'd fallen back. He was about ten yards behind me, riding doubled over in the saddle. I could see the crimson splash on the front of his shirt.

I said, my heart sinking inside me, "Oh, hell!"

I reined up enough to drop back by him. He turned toward me, and I could see how tight he was holding himself against the pain. The way he was doubled over in his saddle I could see where the bullet had gone in from the blood on the back of his shirt. It was just about where the top of his right shoulder blade was. It was a bad place. He was almost certain lung-shot.

A man don't recover very often when he's been lung-shot. Most time his lungs fill up and he drowns in his own blood.

I yelled at him over the hoof-pounding of our galloping horses. I said, "Wilcey, you've got to hold on. We can't stop on this side of the river. But we'll be crossing very soon. Hold on!"

I rode beside, now and again putting out a hand to steady him when it seemed he was getting a little loose in the saddle. Austin had taken up a position on the other side of him and Chulo was now leading.

The road swept very close to the edge of the river and then followed it as it curved. Just around the curve was a narrow place where we'd hardly get the horses wet to their knees as we crossed. We came sweeping around the curve at a gallop. Just ahead was the crossing. I pulled my horse down to a lope and then a trot, yelling at Chulo to do the same. Then when we were at a walk I turned us down toward the river and we went splashing across, Austin and me both being careful that Wilcey was staying in the saddle. Once on Mexican soil I led us back into the interior another mile so we'd be out of sight from the Texas side. I didn't have much idea what kind of pursuit to expect, but for my plan, I wanted them to think we'd crossed into Mexico and headed south.

Of course, my plan was liable to change, with Wilcey being shot. Riding back through the mesquite and the cactus and chaparral, I tried to keep my mind off how

THE TEXAS BANK ROBBING COMPANY

bad he might be hurt. But my heart was just sinking in my breast. I near about couldn't bear to think about Wilcey being hurt. He'd been my partner and my best friend for too long. I didn't know what I was going to do if something happened to him.

After I thought we were far enough back in the boondocks I got us behind a big mesquite clump and dismounted. Then Chulo and I helped Wilcey down. Then I told the Mexican to loosen the cinches on the horses and let them graze off their reins, that we might be there a little while.

I took Wilcey's bedroll off his saddle and then Austin and I helped him over in the shade. I spread the bedroll out and then we set him down on that. The front of his shirt was plenty wet with blood. He was losing a good deal more than he should.

We kept him sitting up. We both knew you did that with a lung-shot. You lay a man down and he'll drown damn quick. He didn't look so bad in the face. While we were getting his shirt off he give me that lopsided grin of his and said, "So I finally done it. Finally got shot."

I said, "Hell, I been shot worse than this when we was just playing."

But it didn't look good. The bullet had come out just above and a little to the side of his right breast nipple. It was a ragged, ugly hole. I glanced up at Austin and he grimaced and shook his head slightly. There was a little pink froth coming out of the hole, which was a bad sign. That's what happened when a man was lung-shot.

Still, Wilcey didn't seem to be breathing all that bad.

He was wheezing a little, but it wasn't that rasping sound I'd expected to hear.

Wilcey said, "Am I lung-shot, Will?"

I glanced at Austin Davis and he pulled a face. But I wasn't all that convinced. I said, "I ain't sure, Wilcey. One way I think you are and another way I ain't so sure. How does it feel when you breathe?"

"Pretty tight," he said. I could see he was starting to get weaker. A good deal of the color had gone out of his face. He tried to laugh, but it didn't come off very good. He said, "Kind of feels like something is loose in there."

Austin said, "We got to get that bleeding stopped."

"Yeah," I said. "There ain't nothing in my saddlebags. You got a clean shirt?"

"Yeah." He got up and came back with a new linen shirt. I tore it into a bunch of strips.

I told Wilcey, "I ain't going to try and doctor it with whiskey against infection until we get the bleeding stopped."

He didn't say anything. I guess it was hurting him pretty bad. I made a couple of pads out of some of the rags and put one over the hole in his back and the one in front. Then while Austin held them in place I wound a long strip around his chest to hold the pads in place and tied it off just as tight as I thought he could stand.

Chulo brought Wilcey's saddle over and we got that behind him, giving him something to lean against. Austin had fetched a bottle of brandy and I mixed some in a cup with a little water and gave it to him. He drank it, but he wasn't much interested. He acted very weak and very listless. I was really feeling bad in my heart. I said, "Wilcey, I'm sorry as hell about this."

THE TEXAS BANK ROBBING COMPANY

He said, "Wasn't nothing to do with you."

I said, "Yeah it was. If I hadn't been so set on robbing that bank, this would never of happened."

He tried another smile, but he was getting too weak to bring it off. He said, "Hell, you always told me we was robbers and our job was to rob. And there was that bank."

God, it was killing me to see him getting so weak. I felt so damn helpless. I said, "You just lay there and take it easy. I got to think what to do."

I got up and walked off a few yards. In a moment Austin Davis joined me. He was carrying the brandy bottle and he handed it to me without a word. I took a drink and then said, "Well, this is a hell of a mess."

He said, "We got to get moving."

I said, "I know it, dammit. But I don't think he's strong enough to ride. I'm thinking of staying here tonight and let him rest up."

Austin shook his head. He said, "You ain't thinking straight. You ain't because he's your good friend. Will, we can't stay here. You know that. They'll have the *Federales* out of Nuevo Laredo looking for us on this side. It's just a matter of time. Stay here and it's jail again. Or worse."

I looked away. "But he's too damn weak to ride. I'm scared he'll bleed to death if I put him back on that horse." God, I was feeling bad.

Austin said, "You know better than that. You know he's going to be weaker tomorrow. And weaker the day after. Right now is as strong as he's going to be for a long time. You know it. It's just that he's your good friend and you can't think right now."

I knew he was right, knew there wasn't a thing I

could say. I said, "I know all of what you say, Austin. But I just can't put him back on that horse. You and Chulo go on and I'll carry him a little farther back in the brush and stay on here until he can travel."

He said, "Now you are talking loco. First off, me and Chulo ain't going to leave. Second, you and him stay here you'll end up in jail and he'll end up dead. Only chance he's got is to get him to a real sawbones. And to do that we got to get way on down this river and then cross over and go back to the Texas side, where they'll be a good doctor. And the sooner we get started the better chance he's got."

I said, "That bullet nicked his lung, didn't it?"

He nodded. "I think it did. By them pink bubbles that was coming out of the hole. Though, to tell you the truth, it ain't sucking air like a bad lung-shot hole does. The one I seen, the air just practically whistled in and out."

I said, "You ever seen anybody make it with a hole in their lungs?"

He shook his head. "Not unless they get to a regular doctor. Something like that can't be handled by the kind of doctorin' you and I know."

I grimaced and took another drink of brandy. "Yeah, I know." Then I shook my head. "Goddammit, why did I have to rob that bank! If I hadn't done that, this wouldn't have happened."

He said, "Aw, hell, Will, you know better than that. Wilcey's already told you. And you know as well as I do that when you're in the kind of business you and I and Wilcey and Chulo are in, you can catch one at any time. You know that's part of the risk. You'd be being a damn fool to blame yourself for him getting shot."

THE TEXAS BANK ROBBING COMPANY

I took another drink and heaved a sigh. "Well, guess I better go over and tell him we got to move on. I don't know how he'll take it."

I walked over and knelt by Wilcey. He was leaned back against the saddle, his arms hugging his chest, staring up at the sky. I offered him the bottle, but he shook his head without saying anything. His breathing was sounding much weaker. It just hurt me to look at him. I said, "Wilcey, we got to go on. We got to get out of this area."

He made a bare little nod. "I know," he said. "Ya'll saddle up and take off."

I said, "No, partner, I mean you too. We ain't leaving you here."

He said, speaking so low I could barely hear him, "I can't, Will. I ain't got the strength. I couldn't ride a hundred yards. Ya'll go on. I'll stay here and rest up."

I said, "There'll be none of that kind of talk. We ain't leaving without you. We been partners too long."

But he just kind of shook his head, weakly. He said, "Will, I can't make it. I'd die within a mile. I know I'm lung-shot. I'd rather just sit here and die. I can't ride."

I said, in a hard voice, "Then you'll die in the saddle. But you damn sure ain't staying here." I looked up. "Chulo, pull up the cinches on the horses. Austin, help me get him up. Chulo, you take his saddle and get it back on his horse."

We got him to his feet while Chulo resaddled his horse. We near about had to carry him over to his horse, so weak had he become. Before we mounted him I made him take a big drink of the brandy. I figured maybe it would give him a little strength. Then it took all three of us to ease him very gently up in the saddle. I tried to think of some way to tie him in the saddle, but there really wasn't any way. I just put both his hands on the saddle horn. "Now you hold onto this. I'm going to take your reins and lead your horse. All you got to do is try and stay on. Chulo, tie his bedroll on behind."

When we were all mounted I led out, leading Wilcey's horse. Austin and Chulo were riding on each side of him, occasionally putting out a hand to keep him steady in the saddle. He just rode with his head down, almost doubled over. I didn't know how long he was going to be able to take it.

I led us out of the mesquite thicket and down toward the river. It would have been easier going in the open land along the river, but we couldn't take the chance. Consequently, I started us southeast about a half mile up from the river, winding us through the mesquite and cactus and all the other thorny plants that chose to live in that harsh country.

Chapter Ten

Judging from the sun, it was pretty close to noon when we were good started on the trail. Fortunately, the ground was pretty level without too many arroyos or cuts. Now and again we'd come to a ravine or a little knob of rocks, but I was able to lead us around these. I don't believe Wilcey could have stood it if we'd of constantly had to be going up and down. As it was all he had to contend with was branches from the low mesquite trees raking up against him.

Still he looked none too good. He had his head down so far that I couldn't see his face, just riding along doubled up, clutched onto that saddle horn with both hands. But I could tell how weak he was from the way his head bobbed up and down, even with the easy motion of his good horse.

One thing, I didn't feel like there was going to be any quick pursuit. The Texas law couldn't cross over to Mexico and it was going to take them more than a little time to get the *Federales* interested and stirred up enough to come looking for us on the Mexican side. And so far as that went, I doubted that anyone had a good idea where we'd headed for. They'd seen us spurring for the International Bridge, but once we were clear of the downtown section I doubt there was two people had seen us cut down the river road. And then we were completely out of sight of the town and could have gone any one of a dozen ways.

And so far as that went, I didn't even know if the sheriff and his deputies had managed to get out of jail yet. If I hadn't of been so worried about Wilcey we'd of all been having a good laugh about the plight of the law.

I looked back and Austin, who had his hand on Wilcey's back, said, "He's doing fine, Will. Let's just keep making tracks."

I was roughly heading for the little town of Zapata, on the Texas side. I figured it would be big enough to have a doctor, for I knew that there was a railroad station and that it was the southern terminus for the train out of San Antonio. Zapata, as well as I could remember, was about sixty miles down river. Had Wilcey not been hurt we could have covered that, by using our good horses hard, in about a day and a half. As it were I figured it would take us closer to three days. I didn't know how Wilcey was going to survive that long, bouncing around in a saddle.

I kept us going for what I judged to be a good three or four hours. Then I led us back into a mesquite clump so we were well hidden and a little shaded from the sun, which was getting pretty warm. I got down and went up to Wilcey's horse.

THE TEXAS BANK ROBBING COMPANY

"Wilcey," I said, "Wilcey." I shook his leg.

He turned his head slowly and looked at me. His eyes were dead and his face was plenty white. I said, "I'm not going to take you down off your horse. We're going to rest here a little while, but we ain't going to be that long and I think it would be harder on you to get off and then have to get back on. But I do want you to take a drink of whiskey. I think it'll make you feel better."

He put out his tongue and licked at his lips. "I want some water first. My mouth is dry."

Austin was standing there. He said, "Sure, I brought two canteens." He went over to his horse and brought one back, unscrewing the cap as he came. Then, while Chulo and Austin held Wilcey upright enough to drink, I held the canteen for him. He gulped down quite a bit and then pulled his mouth away, sighed, and then signaled for some more.

"God, I was dry," he said weakly.

Austin said, "Will, you ought to try and make him eat something. I got a good bit of biscuits and cheese and cold beef I bought at the store early this morning. A piece of that jerky would give him a little strength. And that's all we can do—try and keep his strength up."

Wilcey said, "Will, I can't eat."

"Bullshit," I said. "You've got to eat. I don't want to hear any more about what you can't do."

He said, "Why don't ya'll just leave me here. I'm just slowing you up. This way we're all liable to get caught."

"Yeah," I said. "I'll leave you just like you and Chulo left me and Marianne when she was shot. Now,

223

Wilcey, I don't want to hear any more of that kind of talk. The way you can help the best is to try and do what we think will help you. Like eating this meat Austin has brought you. Now you want me to feed it to you or can you take it in your hand?"

"In my hand," he said. Then with Chulo's help, he straightened enough in the saddle to take the biscuit and meat and slowly chew and swallow it, washing most of it down with water. You could see it hurt him to eat. Hell, for that matter you could see it hurt him to blink his eyes. But he got the meat and biscuit down and then took two big drinks of brandy. It seemed to help him a little. At least some color came back in his face. Not much, but enough to be an encouragement.

I let us rest about half an hour and then put us back on the trail. We went just like we had, me in front with Wilcey's horse on lead, and Chulo and Austin flanking Wilcey.

One thing, the area we were in was a pretty deserted stretch of country. I knew there were no towns on the Mexican side, not even tiny little *pueblas* and damn few ranches. So there were going to be very few observers to mark our passing.

Wilcey appeared to have stopped bleeding. At least I could find no evidence of fresh blood on his bandages when I checked every so often. That was good for his strength, but if he was lung-shot there might not be no way for us to hold him together in time to get him to a sawbones. And then there was the matter of infection. That was generally always the case with a gunshot wound. Unless you got to it in a hurry, which I hadn't, you could near about count on an infection, which usually had about a fifty-fifty chance of killing you.

So my mood was very dismal and low. I didn't like Wilcey's chances at all.

The sun commenced to get low in the western sky. Austin called out that we ought to be looking for a place to camp before it got good dark. I told him I was already looking. The problem with the country was that while its flatness made for easier riding it damn sure didn't provide much cover. We passed a couple of little arroyos with copses of mesquite trees lining them, but they were too shallow. I was hoping to find one deep enough where we could make a fire without danger of it being seen from a distance. Nights in northern Mexico can get mighty cold, no matter how hot it gets during the day, and I figured Wilcey would be running a fever by night so I wanted to do what I could to keep him warm. I also wanted to boil some water and have a go at cleaning up his wound and trying to slow down whatever infection I felt was already gathering.

We kept on, with the sun getting lower and lower. Then, just before I was ready to give up and take whatever came, I spotted a little low mound with a good sized ravine behind it. The mound was toward the river, so, if pursuit was coming from that way, which was likely, it would go further toward blocking off our presence. Besides, the ravine was big enough so that we could get the horses down in its bottom. There was very little grazing for them, but they'd been well rested and well fed for a week, so one night wasn't going to hurt them. Besides, I was willing to bet that Austin had probably thought to bring grain.

We dismounted and then led the horses into the arroyo, taking special care not to jounce Wilcey around too much.

When we were at the bottom we got Wilcey off his horse and laid him out on his sleeping blanket, with his saddle at his back for support. Then I sent Chulo to rustle up some firewood while Austin and I unsaddled the rest of the horses and put them on short picket ropes.

It was just turning dark when we got the fire built. We kept it mighty small, of course, so it wouldn't throw a reflection against the night sky. But the little ravine was lined with mesquite and even a few willows, indicating it sometimes collected water, and I didn't reckon anyone was going to see evidence of us without being mighty close.

Austin seen to getting us all something to eat while I got a skillet we carried, scoured it out with sand, and then put some water on to boil. After that me and Chulo moved Wilcey's sleeping roll over by the fire and then helped him over. He was very weak and was beginning to seem a little feverish, though, ordinarily, the fever and infection don't hit you until the next day.

I figured to put off dressing Wilcey's wound until we'd gotten a little food down all of us. For my part I was bone-weary and just drug down with worry about Wilcey.

We ate some bread and cheese and some cold beef. Wilcey had trouble chewing and swallowing, but he done the best he could and did seem to get enough down to do him some good.

Austin said, "Might be we could fix him up some

THE TEXAS BANK ROBBING COMPANY

beef broth out of that meat. Maybe he could take a little of that some easier."

I nodded. "When I get done dressing his wound with that boiling water we'll fix it back up and make him some broth. Maybe he can take some later tonight or maybe some in the morning."

I knew how much worse he was going to be in the morning and I doubted he'd be able to chew the hard beef and cheese, even if he'd want it, which I knew he wasn't going to.

We sat around for a little while drinking brandy and having a smoke. I wasn't in no rush to get at Wilcey's wound for I knew how bad I was going to have to hurt him to do any good. I kept forcing the brandy bottle on him. He done his best, but he was so weak it was an effort for him just to swallow. It was all he could do to just kind of half sit up, even braced by his saddle as he was. When I'd gotten all the brandy down him I figured he was going to be able to take, I said, "All right, it's time to do it. Chulo, you stoke up that fire a little so I can see a bit better while Austin and I get his shirt off and lay him down."

I'd torn up another shirt of Austin's and had put it in the water as soon as it come to boil. I figured they was plenty purified. I knew they were going to be hot enough.

We got his shirt off and then I unwrapped the bandage from around his chest and took the pads off. Wilcey wasn't breathing too good, just kind of wheezing in and out. I knelt down beside him and put my ear against the hole in the front of his chest. There was a little air coming in and out, but it didn't seem like that godawful amount I'd heard a lung-shot made.

I got Austin to lean down and listen and he kind of nodded. I said, "I don't think he is."

"Maybe it just nicked a corner," Austin said. "And maybe the blood is congealing in the hole to where the air can't get out."

I said, "Well, I'm damn well fixing to find out about that." With the point of my knife I lifted the boiling rags out of the water and held them up in the air to cool. Austin got out his knife and took part of them off my hands so I could work with one rag at a time. I put Wilcey's old bandages in the water to get them purified.

Then, when I thought the rag had cooled enough, I went to scrubbing at the two wounds, washing away the dried blood that had caked on it. Wilcey stiffened and kind of moaned, but didn't make too much commotion.

But, then, the worst was still to come.

By the light of the campfire I kept scrubbing at the wounds until I had gotten the edges good and exposed. They were pretty red, but I figured that was from my doctoring.

I said, "Chulo, hand me that bottle of brandy." Then, to Austin, "We got to lay him back. But I don't want his back wound laying on that dirty blanket. Take that clean rag you got on the point of your knife and kind of hold it over the wound so that it'll be between his back and the blanket."

We got him down and I took the bottle of brandy from Chulo. I said, "Here comes the part he ain't going to like. Chulo, you better get around by his head and hold his shoulders down. Austin, sit on his legs."

THE TEXAS BANK ROBBING COMPANY

Then I just taken that bottle of brandy and forced the mouth into the wound and just let it gurgle in. He stiffened and then he commenced to jerk around and then to kind of cry out.

It was making sweat stand out on my forehead to see the pain he was in. Finally, I jerked the bottle away and took one of the clean rags we'd had in the boiling water and kind of stuffed it down into the wound so it would help it drain. You do that so a wound won't heal over on the outside and then fester on the inside.

After we'd finished with the front, we done the same to the back. Poor Wilcey was so give out from using up what little strength he had jerking around that all he could do was kind of moan real low and just kind of try to lift his head up.

When I was through I put the clean pads back on and then wound the bandage back around his chest, making it tight to stop as much of the new bleeding I'd caused as possible. But I'd been trying to make it bleed a little. That's one way of purifying a wound.

After that we got his shirt back on him and then Austin brought over an extra blanket and we got that over him, laying him down this time with just his head propped up by his saddle. I'd done decided he wasn't lung-shot bad enough to drown to death or he already would have.

But that wasn't saying it wasn't a mighty bad wound. It was.

We was all give out by then. We knew we'd have to have some extra blankets for Wilcey so we made two skimpy beds out of what we had and ended up with three extra to put over Wilcey. I told Chulo to take the first watch for about two hours and then to call me.

Austin said, "Aw, Will, let me take that dog watch. You sleep until I call you. I think you've had the hardest day."

I shook my head. "Naw, I'm all right. I think his worst time is going to be in the middle of the night." I got into my bedroll and Austin got into his. I told Chulo to keep the fire up and to call me at the slightest sign of trouble, either about Wilcey or about anything else.

Then I lay back down, put my head on my saddle, and pulled the blanket up around my neck. Laying there, I realized I hadn't thought much about Marianne, what with worrying about Wilcey and about dodging any pursuit that might be after us. But I was so tired that I just promised myself she was safe in San Antonio and then I went straight to sleep.

They didn't call me for the second watch. Instead, Austin had taken it, having arranged privately with Chulo to do so. Well, I couldn't say I was ungrateful when I crawled out of bed. Chulo was sleeping a few feet away, snoring a bit. I said to Austin, "How's Wilcey?"

He shrugged. "He ain't had too bad a night. He got to shivering pretty bad one time and jerking around a little. But I put them other two blankets on him and it seemed he quieted down."

"Has he been sleeping?"

"Weeelll," Austin said, "I wouldn't call it sleeping so much. He mumbles a little every once in a while. Who the hell was Ruth, by the way?"

I pulled a face. "A goddam worthless woman he

got mixed up with in Houston. I ain't sure, but I think she hurt him worse than that bullet that went through him." I looked up at the moon. It was still a good few hours to dawn. I said to Austin, "You better get to bed, partner. You can still catch about three hours of shut eye."

He yawned and said, "There's coffee in the pot. I just made it fresh about an hour ago."

I nodded and watched while he crawled into the bedroll I'd just got out of. Then I went over and checked on Wilcey. He didn't look so bad. I felt his forehead and it was a little warm, but it could have been warmer.

After that I hunkered down by the fire, poured myself some coffee in a tin cup, and added enough brandy to give it a little bite. I glanced over at the mound Austin made under the blankets. He'd been a damn good friend through all the troubles, and I wasn't going to forget it. But more than a damn good friend, he'd been a cool head and had proven himself to be capable and fearless. He also could think a bit. For if it hadn't of been for him, I had a feeling I might still be enjoying the sheriff's hospitality.

Which gave me a little shock. It seemed like more than yesterday that I'd broken out of jail. It seemed like about a year ago.

I moved over near Wilcey and settled down to wait out the night. I didn't know how we were going to fare on the morrow, but I was going to make him stay alive as long as I could.

For lack of something better to do I got my saddlebag over by the fire and counted the money we'd taken out of the bank. It was a surprising amount, near five thousand dollars. Which hadn't been bad work for such an unplanned job.

But it wasn't near enough to pay for what Wilcey was going through. There wasn't enough money in the world for that.

He started getting bad about an hour before dawn, shivering and shaking, his teeth chattering. I got all the blankets on him I could, tucking them carefully around the edges, but in his fever, he'd thrash around and half throw them off. I spent most of my time kneeling by his side replacing the blankets.

I called Austin and Chulo just as enough light got up to show the little morning mists curling in the bottom of the ravine.

They got coffee and then stood, silently watching me try to keep Wilcey still. Austin said, "Looks like his fever has come up."

"Yeah. It's going to be a bad day. I can already see that. We better get started just as soon as possible. Longer we wait, worse he's going to get."

We all grabbed a quick bite and then Chulo went to get in the horses and get them saddled. Austin had put some meat in the water to get some broth made, but we seen there wasn't any use trying to get any down him. He was nearly out of his head, though he did call for water once just about time we were ready to break camp.

We held him propped up and he drank down a pretty good amount. Then he kind of panted for a moment and then looked up at me. "Will," he said weakly, "when are we going to get to California?"

Austin said, "He's out of his head."

THE TEXAS BANK ROBBING COMPANY

"Yeah, you ought to feel his forehead. He's burning up."

Before we tried to put him on his horse I did coax some brandy down him and then some more water. Me and Austin each got an arm around him, but even with that kind of support he was having trouble walking. And then, at his horse, it took all three of us to get him in the saddle. Austin said, "Listen, Will, he can't ride. He'll fall off in the first five minutes."

I said, worriedly, seeing he was right, "Maybe we can kind of tie him on."

Austin said, "Naw, look, I'm the lightest. I'll get up behind him and hold him on. As slow as we're going his horse can take it for a while. And then we'll switch off to mine."

"Let's try it that way," I said.

Austin got up behind him, putting an arm on each side of him, and then took the reins Chulo handed up to him. He said, "This will be all right."

"Okay, then, let's mount up."

I led us out of the ravine and started southeast again. After we got into easier going I dropped back by Austin. "Look, I'm going to scout on ahead. You just hold to the direction we're heading. I won't be gone but a little."

Then I put spurs to my horse and galloped on ahead, soon losing sight of them in the thick mesquite.

I rode about a mile and then seemed to break into clearer country. After a little farther I suddenly saw a little adobe house upland from the river. I could see several corrals around the main building with a few sorry looking horses standing around with their heads down. It was just the poor adobe shack of a poor

Mexican farmer, but out in front of the house, I saw a little two-wheeled cart. I rode closer. The cart didn't look like much, but I knew we could damn well put it to good use.

I wheeled my horse and headed back for where I thought my partners would be. They had held to the course I'd told them to take and I found them shortly. I pulled them up and then told Chulo what I'd seen and how to find the little rancho. I said, "Now you go up there and you buy that little cart off whoever's home. And buy a horse to put between the shafts and all the harness that is necessary. If nobody is home you get that cart and bring it with you. If they don't want to sell it, you take it away from them."

Chulo laughed. "Choust poor Meskin farmers. Of course, I weel get the *carratera*."

I said, "You pay them for it and you pay them good. We don't want no enemies around here."

He rode off and Austin and I got down and helped Wilcey to the ground. He was calling for water again.

Austin said, "I done put about a gallon in him. That fever must be burning him up."

But it wasn't the fever that was worrying me so much as the way he didn't seem to have no strength or energy. He just kind of fell down wherever we laid him and then didn't even move. We gave him the water and then I tried to get some brandy down him, but I succeeded in getting him to swallow only a very little. He had his eyes open, but he didn't seem to be focusing. And only occasionally would he answer when I tried to talk to him. Finally, we just got him as comfortable as possible and waited for Chulo to come back.

THE TEXAS BANK ROBBING COMPANY

We took the opportunity to eat a little and pass the brandy bottle back and forth and to have a smoke or so. I glanced over at Wilcey every few minutes, but he was just laying there. I knew the country better than Austin so I didn't bother to ask him how he thought we were doing on distance. I myself calculated we'd made about twenty or twenty-five miles since we'd left Laredo. I figured if we could keep pushing we'd be in shape to reach a position across from Zapata the next evening. But other than getting there and getting Wilcey to a doctor, I had no other plans. As I said, the ones I'd made had all gone a-glimmering with Wilcey's injury.

I did, however, ask Austin once more if he felt sure Marianne had gotten on the morning train.

He nodded. "She promised she would. And she said to tell you not to worry, that she'd do as you told her."

Chulo was not long in returning. But he came back alone without the cart. For a moment I thought he hadn't gotten it and I was about to explode before he'd explained he'd tied it up about a quarter of a mile away, being unable to get it through the heavy brush by himself.

We got remounted and set off, having no trouble in finding the cart. It wasn't much, and neither was the bony nag Chulo had bought to pull it. But it was considerably better than what we had and would make traveling a good deal easier on Wilcey.

We got him down and loaded him in the cart, first putting down all the blankets to make a bed and ease his going as best we could. It was just a little two-wheel cart and not quite long enough to hold all of him, but not much more than his boots stuck out the end. There really wasn't a seat for a driver, so Chulo put a rope around the cart horse's neck and took him on lead.

We set off, trying to find the easiest going to get the cart through. We seemed to be making about the same time, but with the cart it was easier all around on men and animals.

I had made no plan as to what to do if we were jumped. It was obvious we couldn't make a run for it with the cart, not all of us. So my plan was to just let each man do what he felt best. On my part I was going to stay with Wilcey and make a fight out of it.

I led us closer down toward the river since the terrain was easier there. I wasn't much worried about pursuit. To be effective, it was going to have to come from the Mexican side and I doubted they'd even bother to look for us this close to the river.

We went on until the sun was about directly overhead and then I led us back upland from the river, found a pretty secluded clump of mesquites, and we made a nooning. We didn't bother to take Wilcey out of the cart or to unsaddle, just loosened cinches and took the bits out of the mouths of the saddle horses so they could graze. Just as I'd figured, Austin had thought to bring grain for the horses. We laid out a bait for each, giving the lion's share to the cart horse, him being by far the poorest and maybe having the hardest job. I knew our horses wouldn't play out, but I wasn't sure about the bony Mexican nag.

As soon as we seen to the horses we got some water boiling over a fire and Austin cut up a little meat in it. We didn't really have much time to make a proper broth, but Austin cut the meat up as fine as he could

THE TEXAS BANK ROBBING COMPANY

and we let it boil about half an hour, making a sort of gruel. Then we raised Wilcey up and I spent about a quarter of an hour trying to get some in him. I finally got him to take a little better than a half a cup. It wasn't much, but I figured every little bit helped.

Chulo done a neat thing. He took his big clasp knife and knocked the top and neck off an empty brandy bottle leaving only the big barrel. We poured the balance of the gruel in there, whittled a stick to the right size, stoppered the bottle with that, and had Wilcey's next meal all ready.

We pushed hard the balance of the day, only stopping occasionally to let the horses rest and, once, to take them down to the river and give them a good watering. The Mexican nag was showing signs of playing out, but we kept feeding him grain along the way and he kept dragging that cart over the rough ground. I wasn't too worried; if he did give out, surely one of our saddle horses could pull the wagon without kicking over the traces.

Wilcey was about the same, either sleeping or unconscious most of the time, only calling out now and again for water. His lips, by now, were so parched and cracked that we had wet a rag and laid it over his mouth. But it really didn't do much good. The burning was coming from inside, from the fever.

Near dark I pulled us back from the river about a mile and found a pretty good campsite. It, too, was down in a little ravine, though not as deep as the other. We found a smooth bank on the back of the arroyo and were able to lead the cart horse down it and get ourselves and all the animals safely on the bottom.

We got a fire built and then we got Wilcey out of the wagon and laid him close, putting as many blankets on him as we could. My only hope was to get him warm enough where his fever would break and, toward that end, I kept trying to get brandy down him.

We ate and warmed up Wilcey's gruel, but he would take even less now. Holding him up with my arm around his shoulder, he was almost hot to the touch. Finally, we just wrapped him up as good as we could and then sat around the fire watching him.

Chulo asked me, "He die, Weelson?"

I flared at him so fiercely I think it almost scared him. "Goddam, no! He ain't going to die! And don't you dare ask me a question like that again, you goddam Meskin, or I'll blow your head off!"

I cooled down in a minute, though. That was just Chulo and he hadn't meant anything by it. To show him I was sorry I passed him the brandy bottle and he had a pull and handed it back to me.

Austin had quit talking about Wilcey. I think he, too, felt he was going to die and just didn't know what to say.

We turned in early, telling off watches. I said, "Ya'll get straight to sleep. We're going to start before light in the morning. I've got to get him to a doctor in a hurry."

The sleep I got was mostly twisting and turning. They could say what they wanted, I still felt responsible for Wilcey. For, if I hadn't caused him to get shot by insisting on robbing that bank, it had still been me who'd led him into outlawry. And he was such a gentle, law-abiding man by nature that he'd no business

THE TEXAS BANK ROBBING COMPANY

in my game. And I should have seen that and not led him down the owl hoot trail.

On my watch I just sat by him and listened to him breathe. Every ragged breath was like a rusty knife in my own chest. It was clear he wasn't getting any better.

We got away early the next morning and had been traveling an hour by the time dawn broke. By now Wilcey would only flicker his eyes open every now and again, without seeing anything, and then close them. What alarmed me was that he'd quit calling for water so, around midmorning, I called a halt and tried to force some down him. He took a little, but it was nip and tuck as to whether it was going to strangle him or go down.

We kept on, now to the accompaniment of the screeching wheels of the buggy which had no grease for several days of hard use. But then we had no grease. Austin tried to wedge a piece of meat between the hubs and the axle, but it did no good and I said to hell with it, we'd just have to put up with the noise.

Then, about mid to late afternoon, we topped a rise, giving us a view over the mesquite, and I saw a town across the river and ahead some two or three miles that had to be Zapata, for there were no more settlements of any size in the area.

We pressed on, me anxious to get to a camping place and send for a doctor before dark.

When I thought we were just about opposite Zapata, I led us back in to the mesquite and hurriedly made a camp, but not building a fire because of our nearness to the town. Then I delegated Austin to go into Zapata and bring a doctor back. It had to be him, for he was the least known of us. I also thought he would be the smoothest at convincing some doctor that he had a hurt comrade who needed his help in a hurry. I made him brush his clothes off and look as respectable as possible and then I hurried him on with the admonition: "He ain't got much time. If the doctor is eating or sleeping or whatever, don't take no delay for an answer. Tell him your friend is laying under a wagon, bad busted up, and can't be moved. Now hurry!"

While he was gone I paced and smoked cigarillos and drank brandy. Chulo sat very quietly watching me. Once he said, "You make yourself seeck, Weelson. You ain't doin' Weelcey any good worryin' so much."

I didn't answer him.

Wilcey was very quiet by now. I just let him alone. I didn't figure there was much more I knew how to do for him.

Then, finally, Austin was there. He was alone and I figured he'd left the doctor down by the river until he could locate the camp. I said, "Where's the doctor?"

He got down before he answered me. He said, "Will, the doctor ain't there. He's gone to San Antonio on the train and won't be back for several days."

"Oh, shit!" I said. I walked a few steps away and then just sat down on the ground and put my head in my hands. I didn't know what else to do. I felt so goddam helpless sitting there with my partner dying and not able to think of a thing to do about it.

Austin knelt down beside me and put his hand on my shoulder. "Maybe he'll come out of it by himself," he said.

THE TEXAS BANK ROBBING COMPANY

I just shook my head. I knew that wasn't true. Wilcey had given up. I'd seen him giving up even before he got shot. He'd commenced giving up when that goddam woman in Houston had run out on him. After that he'd thought nothing good was ever going to happen to him again; he thought he was finished. The only thing that had revived him even a little was when I'd talked about robbing that steamer and getting enough money to make a new start, maybe a ranch for him, maybe a good enough ranch to attract a good woman.

No, he'd given up.

I went over and sat down by him. He was laying so still that, for a moment, I thought he was already dead. I quickly put my ear to his chest. He was still breathing, but just barely. Then, in alarm, I heard what I thought was the death rattle, that dry gurgling sound a man makes with his last breath.

My heart stopped, just as it seemed his breathing did. For a long second I could hear nothing; then it started again, maybe a little weaker this time.

It scared me so bad I took him by the shoulders and said, "Wilcey! Wilcey!" Goddammit, I had to make him come to. I had to make him try and help himself! I shook him a little and called his name louder: "Wilcey! WILCEY! GODDAMMIT! OPEN YOUR EYES! TRY, YOU SONOFABITCH!"

I slapped him in the face once. Then I slapped him again harder and then harder. "WILCEY! OPEN YOUR GODDAM EYES! LISTEN TO ME."

Then I felt Austin's hands under my arms, lifting me up. I guess maybe I was crying a little. He led me off a few yards and handed me a bottle of brandy. I looked down at the ground a minute before I took a quick, long drink. Then I said, "I know. But I don't know what else to do! Goddammit, I don't know of anything to do."

Austin said, "There is one thing. I've seen it done to babies that was down with the colic or the influenza, or whatever it is that babies get."

"What?"

He said, "Well, when it looks like nothing else is going to work, they try and steam that fever out of them. They dig them a hole in the ground and then build a fire in it and put a big bucket of water in there on top of the coals to boil. Then they build a tent over the whole thing and stick the baby in under it and try and steam the fever out. I've seen it work."

I said, "Listen, that—" Then I stopped.

"What?"

"Ah, hell, we ain't got no bucket. We ain't got nothing to make steam in except a little ol' frying pan and that wouldn't make enough steam to wilt a leaf. Shit!"

Austin said, "Riding out from town I seen a washer woman's kettle out in her backyard. Maybe I could go in and get that."

"Do it!" I said. "Go quick! Anything's worth a try. Meanwhile me and Chulo will get the hole dug and a fire built. But hurry!"

Austin took off and I roused Chulo and we attacked the sandy soil with our knives, scraping and digging enough to make a good size hole and one deep enough so the flames wouldn't be a threat to the blankets we'd have to use to make the tent out of. After we had the hole dug we hunted up a quantity of dry mesquite and got a big fire going in the hole, looking for it to make a lot of coals when, and if, Austin got back with the wash pot.

After we got the fire going we cut some long mesquite limbs and teepeed them over the fire, stretching them out enough to make an enclosure big enough to hold a man that was laying down.

Then all we could do was wait. I listened anxiously at Wilcey's chest, expecting every breath to be his last. It was good dark now and we didn't see Austin until he was almost on us. He came riding through the mesquite, balancing a big pot on his saddle horn with one hand and guiding his horse with the other.

I rushed up and took the pot from his saddle and set it on the ground. It was about half full. He said, "That was all I could bring of water. The sucker was near more than I could handle as it was."

We carried it over and set it over the hole. It was just a fit. Then we built up the fire and waited anxiously for the water to boil. When it began to simmer on top we carefully pulled Wilcey over by the fire, having to adjust one of the limbs to get him inside the circle we'd made, and then began peeling the blankets off him and arranging them over the mesquite limbs. The water was boiling good by the time I got the last one in place. Then we took rocks and weighted down the edges where the blanket touched the ground, trying to make it as airtight as possible. I just left one little flap that I could pull back to check on him.

I said, "You reckon he's warm enough in there, just laying on the ground like that with no cover other'n his clothes?"

"Whyn't you see," Austin said.

I pulled the flap back and stuck my head in and it

was steaming plenty good and was mighty warm. I put the flap back and said, "What do we do now?"

Austin said, "I think we just wait."

I said, "How long do we do it?"

He shrugged. "I've seen it done two or three hours, I guess. Course I didn't have no watch."

So we waited. Every once in a while I'd stick my head inside. The steam was so thick I couldn't even see Wilcey, other than his feet, which were right by the flap. I said, "Goddam, can he breathe in there?"

Austin said, "Well, babies can. I guess grown men can too."

I don't know how long we steamed him. But when we heard the last of the water beginning to sizzle in the pot, we decided that was long enough. We took the blankets off, knocked the poles out of the way, and wrapped him back up just as quick as we could. Then we got the pot out of the way and built the fire back up. I said to Austin, "Now what?"

"I guess we wait some more. See what happens."

I sat down by Wilcey's side, kind of pulling one of the blankets up better around his chin. He was soaked, but it was from the steam. He was still breathing, but I couldn't see any change.

God, I was tired, from worry mostly, I figured. I just sat there watching his face and sipping brandy. Finally, I kind of slipped down on one elbow and kind of shut my eyes, which were smarting from the smoke of the fire.

I guess I slept, but I don't know for how long for suddenly a hand was shaking me awake. I jerked up. "What, what! What the hell is it?"

It was Austin. He had a big grin on his face. He said, "He's awake. He's asking for food."

I jumped up and leaned over my partner. He looked mighty weak, but his eyes were open and they damn near looked clear. He said, slowly, "Will, I'm hungry. We got anything to eat?"

I laughed. I laughed and laughed. Then I said, "You sonofabitch, I ought to kill you. You damn near scared me to death!"

Chapter Eleven

It was four days later and we were sitting in the parlor of the big house of Chulo's cousin in San Antonio. Marianne and I were sitting very close together on the settee and Austin Davis was across in a chair with his hat on his knee. Chulo was out, probably chasing every woman in town. His cousin and his cousin's wife were somewhere else in the house. It was cool and comfortable and we had just had a good dinner and were now drinking a little brandy.

Wilcey was down the hall in a bedroom, recuperating. He was still very weak, but he was well on the mend. He was eating well and drinking a little and able to smoke a little and already beginning to worry about this and that. But of course, that was his nature. I was even grateful to hear it, though I knew that would pass shortly and it wouldn't be long before he was irritating the hell out of me with his old woman ways.

THE TEXAS BANK ROBBING COMPANY

We had gotten into San Antonio in early afternoon of that very day and Marianne and I had already hugged and kissed enough so that we were both able to believe that we were together again and we could stand to spend a minute without touching each other. I'd already told her all about it; how we'd made our break and our getaway and Wilcey getting shot and then our desperate flight with him near death. And how, after he'd come to, we'd laid over on the Mexican side for two more days until he'd gotten enough strength back that he could be helped on a horse and make the ride into Zapata. And how there we'd hired out an entire boxcar on the train and loaded ourselves and our animals aboard and then, with plenty of food and drink on board, had ridden like gentlemen right into the railyards in San Antonio.

Austin shook his head. "God, did we get drunk on that damn train! Lord, I ought to have a hell of a head right now, but, somehow, I don't."

I said, "We got a little silly. With Wilcey well and Austin joining the outfit, we got to thinking we were getting so big that we ought to have a name, like the James Gang did or the Hole in the Wall Gang. I wanted to call it the Border Gang, but Austin said it wasn't classy enough. You ought to seen us sitting around in that damn boxcar, drunk as hell, giggling like schoolgirls, trying to come up with a name for a bunch of robbers. Old woman Wilcey said he'd never heard such foolishness from grown men."

She said, "Well, did ya'll ever get a name?"

I shook my head. "Austin claims we have. Of course, *he* was the one made it up. He wants to call us the Texas Bank Robbing Company, like some cafe or grocery store."

That made her laugh a little. "The Texas Bank Robbing Company. That ain't bad."

I said, "I doubt if we ought to advertise or get us a sign. I think we already got enough signs scattered around in different sheriff's offices."

Austin yawned. "If ya'll don't mind, I'm going to hit the hay. I'm about frazzled out."

We didn't mind at all, as matter of fact, since we'd had little enough time alone as it was. He got up. "I'll just see ya'll in the morning. I guess I can find that room Chulo's cousin showed me."

Marianne said, "Good night."

"Yeah," he said. "Ya'll have a good night."

I watched him go out the door. I said, "That's a damn good man. I'm not sure we'd of made it if it hadn't been for him. I know Wilcey wouldn't have if he hadn't of come up with that idea of steaming the fever out of him."

She said, "I felt from the first he was a good man."

I looked at her kind of sourly. "All right, don't start reminding me of that. I'll never be jealous again. Is that good enough?"

She gave me a little hug and we sat quiet for a time. It was good to just relax. Chulo's cousin's house was a good safe place. He was a receiver of stolen cattle, but his arrangements with the law were such that they'd never come in his residence; he was too important a thief and paid off too many politicians for that to happen. Of course, it wouldn't do, not as hot as we were, to be walking the streets, but for the time being, we were safe enough where we were.

THE TEXAS BANK ROBBING COMPANY

Marianne said, "Will, you scared me to death, getting yourself in that jail. I don't know how much of that I can take."

I looked at her. "It may happen again. Do you want out? You know how risky my business is. You better think about it."

She shook her head, hard. "No, I don't want out! And don't say that to me again. I'm a big girl and I come in this with my eyes wide open. I'm a woman and, from time to time, I'm allowed to say I ain't sure I can take much more. Goddammit, don't you ever ask me if I want out again!" She hit me on the arm. "Ain't I allowed to be scared? Wasn't you scared?"

I laughed a little. "Oh, I guess so. Maybe a bit."

Then we were quiet again, just kind of holding on to each other. After a little she said, "Well, what's next for the Texas Bank Robbing Company?"

I smiled, but then I shook my head. "I don't know. For sure stay here and rest up for a week or so and let Wilcey get well and strong. After that I ain't got no idea. One thing—" I looked at her. "I'd like to try and talk Wilcey into getting out of this business. He ain't cut out for it and he's going to worry me the rest of the time. I'd like to see him change his range. Head up north somewheres. Maybe to Montana." Then I stopped. "But of course, he hasn't got the money right now to get back in the ranching business." I grimaced. "But I guess we don't have enough to make a change either. How much we got now?"

She said, "Well, with what you brought in off that idiotic robbery you pulled in Laredo, about six thousand dollars."

I said, "That ain't much. Not much to make any big plans off of."

"So what are we going to do?"

I said, "I guess pull one more robbery to get enough." Then I shrugged. "But of course I been pulling just one more robbery for years."

"Is there ever going to come a time when one more robbery is the last one?"

I looked at her. "You want the truth?"

"I always want the truth."

"Will it scare you?"

She said, "It may scare me, but it won't change anything between you and I."

I said, "Then, I reckon not. I reckon I'm a bank robber by trade. And a payroll robber and a train robber. I reckon that's what I'll always be." I smiled at her. "You want to make a toast to that?"

So we each picked up our glasses, said "Luck" and then knocked them straight back as befits the toast.

America's #1 bestseller
by the author of
SHŌGUN, TAI-PAN, and KING RAT

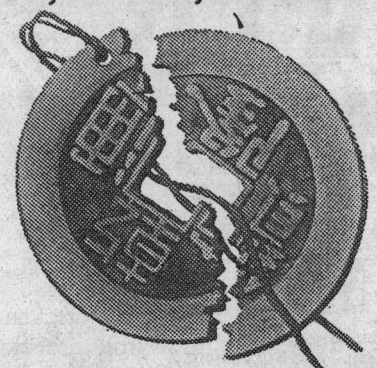

JAMES CLAVELL'S
NOBLE HOUSE

"Breathtaking. Only terms like colossal, gigantic, titanic, incredible, unbelievable, gargantuan are properly descriptive. Clavell has made himself the king of super-adventure thrillers."—*Chicago Tribune Book World*

A Dell Book $5.95   (16483-4)

At your local bookstore or use this handy coupon for ordering:

| Dell | DELL BOOKS
P.O. BOX 1000, PINE BROOK, N.J. 07058-1000 | NOBLE HOUSE $5.95   (16483-4) |

Please send me the above title. I am enclosing $_____ (please add 75c per copy to cover postage and handling). Send check or money order—no cash or C.O.D.'s. Please allow up to 8 weeks for shipment.

Mr./Mrs./Miss_____

Address_____

City_____ State/Zip_____

Over 2½ months on the *New York Times* Bestseller List!

PAPER MONEY

by ADAM SMITH

The bestselling author of *The Money Game* and *Supermoney*, Adam Smith, a noted economist, reveals what happened and what will happen to the dollar, real estate values and the stock market. Never has he been more needed than in a time when inflation and confusion are both soaring.

"Adam Smith simplifies economic theory without being condescending. Before there is a run of the bank, there should be a jog to the bookstore."—*Time*

A DELL BOOK $3.95   (16891-0)

At your local bookstore or use this handy coupon for ordering:

| **Dell** | DELL BOOKS
P.O. BOX 1000, PINE BROOK, N.J. 07058-1000 | **PAPER MONEY** $3.95 (16891-0) |

Please send me the above title. I am enclosing $_____ (please add 75¢ per copy to cover postage and handling). Send check or money order—no cash or C.O.D.'s. Please allow up to 8 weeks for shipment.

Mr./Mrs./Miss_____

Address_____

City_____State/Zip_____

A Saint Patrick's Day you'll never forget!

Cathedral
by NELSON De MILLE

Terrorists seize St. Patrick's Cathedral, threatening the lives of hostages. Can someone avert the catastrophe that could destroy world peace?

"Dazzling. I'll never walk by St. Paddy's again without wondering whether there is a sniper in the bell tower and never go inside without glancing nervously at the choir loft."—Father Andrew M. Greeley, author of *The Cardinal Sins*

"A riveting suspense novel. Vivid characterizations. A perfect blending of plot and people."—Robert J. Serling, author of *The Presidents Plane Is Missing*

A DELL/BERNARD GEIS ASSOCIATES BOOK $3.95   (11620-1)

At your local bookstore or use this handy coupon for ordering:

Dell DELL BOOKS   CATHEDRAL $3.95 (11620-1)
P.O. BOX 1000, PINE BROOK, N.J. 07058-1000

Please send me the above title. I am enclosing $_____ (please add 75c per copy to cover postage and handling). Send check or money order—no cash or C.O.D.'s. Please allow up to 8 weeks for shipment.

Mr./Mrs./Miss_____

Address_____

City_____State/Zip_____

The National Bestseller!

GOODBYE, DARKNESS

by WILLIAM MANCHESTER
author of *American Caesar*

The riveting, factual memoir of WW II battle in the Pacific—
and of an idealistic ex-marine's personal struggle to understand
its significance 35 years later.

"A strong and honest account, and it ends with a clash of
cymbals."—*The New York Times Book Review*

"The most moving memoir of combat in World War II that I
have read. A testimony to the fortitude of man. A gripping,
haunting book."—William L. Shirer

A Dell Book $3.95   (13110-3)

At your local bookstore or use this handy coupon for ordering:

Dell   DELL BOOKS   GOODBYE, DARKNESS $3.95   (13110-3)
P.O. BOX 1000, PINE BROOK, N.J. 07058-1000

Please send me the above title. I am enclosing $_____ (please add 75c per copy to cover postage and handling). Send check or money order—no cash or C.O.D.'s. Please allow up to 8 weeks for shipment.

Mr./Mrs./Miss_____

Address_____

City_____ State/Zip_____

"A hard, cruel, cynical novel—
and a good one."—
The Washington Post Book World

HORN OF AFRICA

by Philip Caputo

author of *A Rumor of War*

Three mercenaries embark on a reckless mission to turn a tribe of warriors into a modern army. Caught in the fanaticism of mad war, thrust beyond the reach of civilization, they crossed the boundaries of conscience and confronted war's bottomless capacity for violence and evil.

"Shades of Joseph Conrad and Graham Greene."—*Booklist*

A Dell Book $3.95   (13675-X)

At your local bookstore or use this handy coupon for ordering:

Dell | DELL BOOKS   HORN OF AFRICA $3.95   (13675-X)
P.O. BOX 1000, PINE BROOK, N.J. 07058-1000

Please send me the above title. I am enclosing $_____ (please add 75c per copy to cover postage and handling). Send check or money order—no cash or C.O.D.'s. Please allow up to 8 weeks for shipment.

Mr/Mrs./Miss_____

Address_____

City_____ State/Zip_____

SOLO

by **JACK HIGGINS**
author of The Eagle Has Landed

The pursuit of a brilliant concert pianist/master assassin brings this racing thriller to a shattering climax in compelling Higgins' fashion.

A Dell Book $3.25   (18165-8)

At your local bookstore or use this handy coupon for ordering:

Dell	DELL BOOKS	SOLO $3.25 (18165-8)
	P.O. BOX 1000, PINEBROOK, N.J. 07058	

Please send me the above title. I am enclosing $_____
(please add 75¢ per copy to cover postage and handling). Send check or money order—no cash or C.O.D.'s. Please allow up to 8 weeks for shipment.

Mr/Mrs/Miss _____

Address _____

City _____ State/Zip _____